D1391906

NURSE MATILDA GOES TO HOSPITAL

by Christianna Brand
illustrated by Edward Ardizzone

To darling Lucy
and to Danny and Joel
and to all the other children
who know that I am a whych

Published in Great Britain in 2005 by Bloomsbury Publishing Plc
38 Soho Square, London, W1D 3HB

First published in 1974 by The Brockhampton Press Ltd

Text copyright © 1974 Christianna Brand
Illustrations copyright © 1974 Edward Ardizzone
The right of Christianna Brand to be identified as the author of this work has been asserted by the Estate of Christianna Brand in accordance with the Copyright, Designs and Patents Act, 1988
The right of Edward Ardizzone to be identified as the illustrator of this work has been asserted by the Estate of Edward Ardizzone in accordance with the Copyright, Designs and Patents Act, 1988

All rights reserved
No part of this publication may be reproduced or transmitted by any means, electronic, mechanical, photocopying or otherwise, without the prior permission of the publisher

A CIP catalogue record of this book is available from the British Library

ISBN 0 7475 7678 5

Printed and bound in Italy by Artegrafica S. p. A. Verona

1 3 5 7 9 10 8 6 4 2

All papers used by Bloomsbury Publishing are natural, recyclable products made from wood grown in well-managed forests. The manufacturing processes conform to the environmental regulations of the country of origin.

Chapter 1

NCE upon a time there were a mother and father called Mr and Mrs Brown and they had lots and lots of children; and all the children were terribly, terribly naughty.

One wintry Sunday, Mrs Brown went up to the schoolroom to speak to her children and this is what they were doing:

Tora had fastened a melting icicle to the back of Nanny's skirt and everywhere Nanny went she found, to her great alarm, that she was leaving a little wet dribble.

Jake had nailed a bit of fish to the underneath side of the big round schoolroom table and no one could think where the awful smell was coming from.

Joel had put glue in the girls' woolly outdoor gloves and now, however much Nanny crossly told them to take them off, the poor things couldn't.

All the other children were doing simply dreadful things too.

Mrs Brown was very sweet but she really was rather foolish about her dear, darling children, and never could believe that they could be really naughty. So she said: 'Good morning, Nanny, I hope the children are behaving themselves?'

'Yes, Madam,' said Nanny gloomily, hoping Mrs Brown wouldn't notice the little dribble or the strong smell of fish or the fact that all her daughters appeared to have developed large, hairy, coloured hands.

'Well, then, children, I have a lovely surprise for you,' said Mrs Brown. 'What do you think? Nurse Matilda is coming to tea.'

Some of *you* children will have read about how Nurse Matilda came to the naughty Brown children and made them all good again. She was dreadfully ugly but as they got gooder and gooder, she got prettier and prettier until at last she was really lovely and all surrounded by a sort of golden glow. But I'm afraid that when she went away, the children always got naughty all over again.

However, they were delighted that she was

coming to see them. 'We had better not go to Sunday School,' they said, piously, 'but stay at home and put on our best clothes for Nurse Matilda.'

'Beck cloag for Nurk Magiggy,' echoed the Baby. It was a splendid baby and talked a language all of its own. It wore an untidy bundle of nappies which always looked as though they were going to come down, but never quite did.

'That will be lovely,' said Mrs Brown, very proud that they should have thought of putting on their best clothes, which they loathed – and quite right too, because they were simply hideous. 'But I think you'll be able to fit in Sunday School too.'

'Oh, *lor'*!' said the children, not piously at all.

So after midday dinner, they formed into a long crocodile and went off through the snow to the church hall, driven from behind by Nanny; (her boots had by now filled with water from the melted icicle and she was very uncomfortable and couldn't make it out at *all*). The village children stood by to cheer them on their resentful way, led by their greatest enemy, a large and horrible boy called Podge Green; all leaping up and down sticking out their tongues and calling out, 'Yah-yah – goody-goodies!' 'You just wait!' muttered the crocodile, filing by, showing all its teeth.

The Vicar, whose name was Mr Privy, had planned a little lecture about Loving Thy Neighbour, and had even made up a special hymn, beginning, '*Children who are kind and meek, And always turn the other cheek, Will fill their lives with merry fun, And be belov'd by everyone.*' He sometimes felt that it was not very likely that the Brown children would ever be belov'd by everyone, or even anyone at all, especially by himself. However, he had even made up a tune to go with his hymn and all the mothers and children in the class stood up to sing it.

The Brown children, however, who perhaps were not quite so kind and meek as they should have been, always sang whatever hymn they chose and that was what finally won; for they simply sang away, never mind what music was being played or what the other people were singing, and there were so many of them that in the end everyone else gave up and joined in with *them*. So they now sang Onward Christian Soldiers at the tops of their voices, and this, I must say, did make it rather a bad start for Mr Privy and his little talk about living at peace with one's neighbour; especially, he thought to himself, if one's neighbour was the Browns.

He embarked upon it at last, however, with a look towards them that suggested that he might profit by the lesson himself. The children gazed back at him with innocent faces, meanwhile keeping up a muffled underground hullabaloo, the boys playing a kind of soccer with their caps between the rows of chairs, the girls poking under the seats with their umbrellas at the legs of the people in front of them . . . 'Emma! Susie! Tim! Be-*have*!' hissed Nanny, squelching angrily up and down the aisle with her boots full of water.

Clemency stood up in her place. She said to Mr Privy in a very loud, clear voice, 'I can't hear what you're saying?'

Charlotte shot up in *her* place. 'Neither can I.'

'Neither can we,' cried all the Brown children.

'Oh, dear, that will never do! I'll try to speak louder,' said Mr Privy. He proceeded on his discourse in a rousing bellow. 'We still can't hear,' complained the children, bellowing back.

Poor Mr Privy threw a great deal of expression into his words, twisting his poor face into knots in his effort to make himself understood. 'He looks like a mad horse,' whispered Jennifer. All along the rows of seats, the children burst into muffled giggles, passing the message along. 'Ara*bella*! Cla*rissa*! Se*bas*tian!' hissed Nanny, dashing squelch, squelch from one side of the aisle to the other, 'I said *bee-have*!'

'Why does she keep saying bee-hive?' said Roger. Goodness, he added thoughtfully, suppose there was a swarm of bees!

'A swarm! Ow-ow!' cried all the children immediately. 'A swarm of bees! Nanny says there's

a swarm of bees!' and they flapped their hands in front of their faces to drive away the imaginary bees.

'Bees?' cried the lady in the front bench, turning round with an anxious look.

'Yes, bees. And, excuse me,' said Christianna, politely, 'but you've got one too. You've got a bee in your bonnet,' and she leaned forward and kindly tried to brush the bee off. But she only succeeded in brushing off the bonnet and several bits of the lady's hair with it. 'Look out, look out!' cried the Little Ones helpfully, in high shrill voices. 'A bee will sting your bald head!' The lady clapped back the bonnet, bits of hair and all and, holding it on with one hand, flapped wildly round the heads of her own children. 'Lucy, Thomas, Victoria, William! Be careful, you'll get stung. . .!' The children next to Lucy and Thomas and Victoria and William began to flap too, passing on the alarming news . . . The Brown children set up a steady, humming bzz-bzzzz.

Up on the platform, Mr Privy, deafened to all this sound and confusion by his own attempt to shout loud enough, stopped at last and peered down over the tops of his glasses. His whole

Sunday school seemed suddenly to have gone mad: rising up in their seats and dancing about in the most extraordinary fashion, waving their arms above their heads with looks of extreme terror on their poor pale faces. Several of those dreadful – those *dear, sweet* Brown children, said Mr Privy to himself, remembering just in time his own talk about loving your neighbour – had got hold of the little black velvet butterfly nets on the ends of long sticks which were used in the church next door to collect the Sunday offerings – and were chasing up and down swatting at the air with increasingly unbridled cries of, 'Missed it!' and 'Got it!' – and rushing to the windows and shaking something out of the bags and dashing back for more. 'Got *what*?' cried poor Mr Privy, peering this way and that. 'Bees!' cried the audience back to him. 'A plague of bees! The whole place is swarming with them, take care, you'll get stung!' And they began to leap up and down more agitatedly than ever at the idea of their own dear Vicar a prey to bees, and to cry out to the children with the butterfly nets to rescue him.

'Rescue the Vicar! Rescue Mr Privy!' cried the

Brown children, delighted at the idea. With Pam and Simon in the lead, half a dozen of them crept up on to the platform. Simon took a great swipe.

The velvet bag was not very strongly sewn on, for it came away quite easily from its ring and remained sitting on top of Mr Privy's head like a little black nightcap. The ring, still on its long handle, went on down round his neck. He said in a voice by no means filled with love for Simon: 'GET – IT – OFF!'

The children hung on to their end of the handle and tried to get the ring off: but the ring wouldn't come. They pulled it this way, and nearly flattened Mr Privy's nose against his face, they pushed it that way and half lifted him off his feet by the ears – but it wouldn't come. Caro said at last: 'We shall have to get some soap.'

'Soap?' choked the Vicar. The metal ring had got lodged between his teeth now, like a horse's bit.

'To make your face more slidey,' explained Lindy kindly.

So Christianna produced some soap from the vestry next door and they soon had a fine lather all over Mr Privy's face; snowflakes of it drifted about the room as he puffed and blew, struggling like anything to get away from their kind ministrations. They had to give up in the end and, leading him like an angry little bull at the end of a rigid halter, got him down from the platform and disappeared with him into the vestry. Muffled cries of 'Ow! Ow!' echoed through the hall – at first from Mr Privy and then, I am sorry to say, from the children. I don't think Mr Privy had profited one bit from his own lesson about loving everybody. After all, they were only trying to rescue him from the bees.

Meanwhile, Podge Green and his friends had been waiting at the lych gate of the church, rather anxious and beginning to wish they had not pulled the crocodile's tail quite so hard. 'We must arm ourselves with lots of snowballs,' said Podge, assuming the leadership in a very important manner.

It seemed a long time before the children came out of the church hall, and in fact it was. The Vicar, muttering urgently to himself that he must try to love his neighbour even if it was one of the Browns, was standing in the doorway shaking hands with all the mothers and children as they passed out, and speaking a kindly word. The Brown children, eager to see how long he could keep this up, were filing by and immediately running round and re-joining the end of the queue. By the time he had shaken hands four times each with every one of them, and spoken a fourth kind word, he was – though much delighted at such a large attendance to his Sunday School – getting tired and rather cross. And so was Nanny, who had to keep running round after her charges and getting her hand shaken and a kindly word, time after time; when all she wanted to do was to chivvy them all home and change into dry boots.

Podge Green and his army stood beside their fine big heaps of snowballs. 'Here they come!'

This time Nanny was in the lead with the Little Ones trotting behind her, holding hands in angelic pairs. The first snowball took her bonk! on the nose and was followed by such a hail of snow that when she looked back, the babies had entirely disappeared and there was only a long, white, writhing monster uttering muffled cries of 'Let us *out*!' So much occupied was she in dashing up and down brushing the snow off the tops of their heads, that she did not see that Podge's army was in full flight down the hill pursued by the Middling Ones and the Big Ones of the Brown family.

Podge Green's mother and father ran the sweet shop in the village and Podge and his friends ate far too much biscuit and chocolate and were all very fat; though none was nearly as fat as Podge himself. Being so stout, they couldn't run very fast and soon fell over their own feet and went rolling off down the hill, gathering snow as they went, until they were nothing but huge, round snowballs themselves – spinning at a great rate and ending up with a bonk against the wall at the bottom. But Podge was *so* fat that his head and feet were right up off the ground and he finished up like a sort of rolling-pin, with his head and feet like the rolling-pin handles, sticking out at both ends. Upon these ends the Brown children seized joyfully and, leaving the others lolling like broken snowmen against the wall, they trundled him through the village towards their own gate.

The snow had melted here and little bits of gravel from the road stuck to Podge as he rolled. By the time they came to the top of their drive, he looked as if he had been egg-and-breadcrumbed, all ready to be fried. He could have done with some frying, as a matter of fact. 'Ow, ow!' he cried. 'I'm *cold*!'

'I expect your blood is frozen in your veins,' said the children standing round him cheerfully. 'We shall have to make a hole in you and light a little fire and boil it up a bit,' and they trundled the rolling-pin round to the back door and began to haul and push it, melting rapidly, up the back stairs. Hoppit the butler and Cook, and Hortense the lady's maid, and Alice-and-Emily the parlour maids, would be safely out of the way having a Sunday afternoon snooze; ('Drat that Nanny!' said Cook later to Hoppit, 'she must have dribbled the whole way up them back stairs. They're all wet. Whatever can be the matter with her?')

The children got Podge into the schoolroom and heaved him up, stiff as a board, on to the table. 'We shall need some very large kitchen knives to cut him open with,' said Stephanie. 'And some boiling water to unfreeze his inside with,' said Sarah. 'And some needles and cotton to sew him up again,' said Sophie. 'Or what about some glue?' said Hetty. 'Ow, ow, *ow*!' said Podge.

So Fenella went down to the kitchen and returned with some of Cook's aprons and Dominic made some of Hortense's stiff, starchy white caps into splendid surgeons' masks, and Christopher, who was not exactly a good speller, went outside and with a piece of chalk drew a large red cross on the schoolroom door and wrote in big letters: HOSPIDILT. '*Now*!' they said to Podge.

And at that moment from outside came Mrs Brown's voice, saying, 'Children? Have you forgotten you're expecting a visitor?' And the door flew open. And there she stood, smiling and lovely and all in her golden glow. Nurse Matilda!

'Nurk Magiggy!' cried the Baby joyfully. 'Ick my Nurk Magiggy!' 'Oh, yes,' cried all the children. 'It's Nurse Matilda!'

Nurse Matilda took one look around her – at the girls in their nurses' aprons, at the boys in their surgeons' masks – at Podge lying trussed up in a pool of melting snow and little stones; at the notice on the door. And the glow went out; and suddenly Nurse Matilda wasn't pretty any more – but a small, stout, ugly person carrying a big black stick – what Nurse Matilda could do with that

big black stick! She wore a rusty black dress that came up to her neck and right down to her black button boots, and a rusty black bonnet all trembly with jet, with the bun of her hair sticking out at the back like a teapot handle. And her face was very brown and wrinkly and her eyes were very small and black and shiny; and her nose! – her nose was like two potatoes. But what you noticed most of all about her was her Tooth – one huge front tooth, sticking right out like a tombstone over her lower lip . . .

'*Well!*' said Nurse Matilda. And she lifted up her big black stick and gave one thump on the schoolroom floor.

Chapter 2

BANG! went the big black stick; and all of a sudden there came a clanging of bells and rattling of wheels over the frozen roads, and a scuttering of gravel as horses' hooves pulled up on the drive beneath the schoolroom window; and great cries of 'Get out the stretchers! Where's the medicine! Have some bowls ready in case they're sick!' And the children looked at each other and looked down their own fronts – and saw that everyone was in a dressing-gown and bedroom slippers, with a neat little parcel of washing things in one hand.

And they looked out of the window and there, lined up before the front door, was a whole fleet of horse-drawn ambulances. And they knew that the worst had happened. They had teased poor fat Podge about being in hospital and now Nurse

Matilda had banged with her big black stick – and here they were in dressing-gowns all ready to go into hospital themselves!

'Or going inkoo hokkigig?' said the Baby, raising its wondering big blue eyes to Nurse Matilda. 'In our jenking-gowns?'

Nurse Matilda looked down at it and just for a moment she smiled a tiny little smile; and she lifted up the Baby in her arms and stood with it held close and safe against her rusty black shoulder – and moved back and out of the way. And in through the door poured a horde of white-coated men who snatched the children up in pairs and laid them on to stretchers and scurried off down the stairs and hoisted them into ambulances and dashed back again for more. 'Hey, what are you doing? – there's nothing wrong with *us*!' cried the children, anxiously. 'Tonsils this lot!' cried the stretcher-bearers over their heads, taking no notice; or, 'Appendicitis, these three!' or, 'Medical wards, those ones there, they only need lots of Doses . . .!' 'No we don't,' cried the children, 'we're perfectly well, we don't need operations and we certainly don't need Doses!' They had in the past had experience of Nurse Matilda's medicine.

But nobody took any notice. Soon the attendants climbed in, one to each ambulance, and the doors were slammed shut and off they went, the horses clattering gaily down the drive and out through the village, with the children bumping resentfully behind. 'Well, there's one thing,' they said to each other, 'when we get to the hospital, Nurse Matilda won't be there with her big black stick. You don't have children's nurses in hospitals.' And they began to think of naughty things to do when they got there.

In fact, they could think of some naughty things to do right now . . . 'Ow! Ow!' cried all the children in the leading ambulance. 'Stop the ambulance, quick!'

'What for?' cried the ambulance men, alarmed.

'Ow! Ow!' cried the children, not answering directly. 'Stop the ambulance, stop the ambulance!'

So the ambulance stopped and the ambulances behind it had to stop too; and in a minute the children had all jumped out and were seizing the ambulance men and tying them up with bandages and lying them down on the bunks, well wrapped up in red hospital blankets; and

Anthony and Edward and Justin had jumped up on the driving seats and were saying 'Chk, Chk!' to the horses and hoping they would just trot on ahead which, being nice horses, was what they did.

The hospital was a very big white building full of tidy white beds, hungry for patients. But the people who lived all round seemed to be dreadfully healthy and lots of the beds were empty. The surgeons and doctors and nurses were simply longing for more people to chop up and dose and tuck into the tidy white beds; and quite a cheer arose from the Staff, assembled on the wide front steps as the first of the ambulances appeared.

Eager hands pulled open the doors and lifted out the stretchers. 'M'f,m'f,m'f,' cried the occupant of the first stretcher in an angry voice muffled by tightly tucked-in red blankets. 'Don't you worry, everything will be quite all right,' said the hospital porters, humping the stretcher cheerfully up the steps. 'M'f,m'f,*m'f!*' insisted the patient desperately. 'Oh, they all say that, but you'll simply love it really,' cried all the nurses and surgeons and doctors; and, terrified that one of their victims would rebel and jump up off the stretcher and get away, they all helped to bundle it on to a sort of thing on wheels and bowl it away down the corridor. 'Immediate operation!' panted the ambulance attendant, lolloping along, keeping pace with it, though he kept falling over his white coat which seemed to be much too long.

'No time to waste!' 'Emergency!' cried all the surgeons joyfully and began to race one another down the long corridors, pulling on their brown rubber gloves as they went. '*M'f,m'f,M'F!*' yelled the poor patient through mouthfuls of red blanket.

The surgeon who got there first was the top one of the lot; his name was Sir Minsupp Izgizzard. He took no notice at all of m'f,m'f, m'fs, but seized up a huge knife and was just about to chop up the patient right, left and centre when he suddenly remembered that he didn't know what was wrong with him. 'What's wrong with you?' he said.

'*M'f*-m'f,' said the patient.

'It can't be nothing or you wouldn't be here. Now take that thing out of your mouth,' said Sir Minsupp impatiently, 'and tell me plainly what's the matter.' But he now observed that the patient's arms were tightly strapped down to his sides and he hastily unbuckled them. 'Good heavens!' he said. '*You're* not a patient. You're the ambulance attendant. Why didn't you say so?' And he dropped everything and rushed back to the front door steps. 'Look out!' he cried. 'They're up to mischief! Don't let any of them get away . . .!'

All the surgeons and the doctors and the nurses turned round to hear what he was saying. By the time they turned back again, another patient had been carried up on a stretcher; and a rather small coachman in a very large coachman's hat and coat was driving away the second ambulance. 'M'f, m'f, m'f!' cried the patient. 'I've heard that before! Follow that ambulance!' cried Sir Minsupp. Out of the ambulance windows peered the faces of a dozen children all crammed in for the get-away. 'Oh well,' they said to each other, as the surgeons and nurses and doctors caught up with them, 'we'll have to think of something naughty to do once we're *in*.' They thought they might just manage to think of something.

I think the last ambulance-full of children were really the best – or the worst, I suppose I ought to say. When Sir Minsupp Izgizzard finally got the patient on to the operating table – after the most fearful struggle going on under the red blankets and M'f,m'f,m'fs in the most *extraordinary* voice – he discovered (only just in time) that he was taking out the tonsils of one of the ambulance horses! (The horse simply loved it and ever afterwards bored all the other horses by insisting upon telling about 'my operation'.)

By supper time, the hospital had more or less settled down again. The ambulance men had been sorted out and were conducting a meeting about how they could all get different jobs, the horse was back in the stables making dreadful puns about, 'I kept telling them I was only a little hoarse, but they still took out my tonsils . . .' and the Brown children were tucked up among various other patients in several wards.

All the wards – fortunately for the children – radiated off a sort of central hall, like the spokes of a wheel; so they weren't too far from each other. Podge Green had been gathered up with the rest of them and was in a corner bed stodging down the hospital supper which was simply horrible fish and rice pudding – to Podge any food was better than no food; and the Baby had a little cot where it spent its time standing up watching everything over the top rail, with its nappies coming down round its fat, bent knees as usual.

When Staff Nurse arrived to announce Matron's Round, this is what the children were doing:

Joanna had scraped up the uneaten rice pudding from all the plates and stuffed it into a spare pillow case.

Louisa and Rebecca had collected the bunches of grapes which the patients' kind relatives had brought them, and were treading them into wine in a hospital hip-bath.

Daniel had swapped round all the charts at the heads of the patients' beds which told what was wrong with them, and added a few suggestions of his own.

Romilly had turned the Little Ones' cots upside down and made sort of wooden cages out of them; and the Little Ones were pretending to be in a zoo.

All the other children were doing simply dreadful things too.

Staff Nurse was very round and red and when she was cross she could give a very loud bellow. She gave a very loud one indeed when she saw Rebecca and Louisa treading wine in the middle of her ward. They skipped pretty quickly back into bed, with their feet bright purple from the grapes. 'All sit up straight and tidy,' said Staff Nurse. 'Matron will be making her Rounds.' She caught up the temperature chart of one of the elderly patients. 'A hundred and four! What are you sitting up for? You'll kill yourself.'

'You told me to,' said the patient. 'You've just said to sit up straight.'

'Well then, lie down straight,' said Staff Nurse, crossly. She whipped up another chart. 'My goodness, Mrs Bloggs, you *are* getting better! You can jump up and help to clear away the supper trays.'

Of course poor Mrs Bloggs's chart had been mixed up by Daniel with somebody else's. 'I can't,' she said, reeling round and round in little circles, quite dizzy with temperature. 'My head's buzzing like a bee-hive.'

'Nonsense,' said Staff Nurse. 'You mustn't imagine things. It says here on your chart that you're perfectly normal.' She marched off into one of the boy's wards. 'Eaten up all your nice supper? Good! All nice and comfortable?'

'Ibe dot,' said Podge. He was still very chilly from being made a rolling-pin out of, and had already developed a cold in his nose. 'I'be very *ud*cubfortable.'

'Nonsense!' said Staff Nurse again. Nobody was allowed to be uncomfortable in *her* ward. 'Here – have another pillow!' She picked up one that seemed to be spare and put it behind his head with an angry pat. 'Matron will be round in a minute and I want you all to be enjoying yourselves. *En-joying* yourselves,' she repeated glaring round at them, daring them to feel ill or miserable.

'Yes, Nurse,' said the patients obediently, though they felt that they might be going to enjoy themselves even less now that the Brown children had arrived. 'You will love Matron,' they added to the children, hoping to impress them all into good behaviour. 'So kind –'

'So gentle –'

'Florence Nightingale herself –'

And here was Matron, bearing down upon them along the corridor like a liner coming into port with sisters and nurses and junior doctors like little tugs, fussing around her; hooting Yes Matron, No Matron, as they advanced. 'Well, Staff Nurse – everything going smoothly?'

'Yes Matron, No Matron,' said Staff Nurse, catching the infection. They all came to a halt in the little central hall and Matron turned slowly round and looked down the long length of each of the wards. 'Um – not exactly *smoothly*, Matron,' said Staff Nurse, making up her mind.

'H'm,' said Matron spinning slowly to look into the first ward.

Mrs Bloggs was still spinning. She had got out of bed, as instructed by Staff Nurse, and was now going round and round in little circles, carrying a supper tray and buzzing away happily to herself, her face quite crimson with high temperature but very glad to have been told by Staff Nurse that she was perfectly well. Further down the ward, however, an anxious lady called Miss Fizzle was lying back against her pillows in a terrible taking because *her* temperature had apparently shot up to a hundred and four. She had struggled up and read the chart at the head of her bed and besides having all Mrs Bloggs's troubles listed on it, the children had added a few suggestions of their own. Over opposite, a stout old lady also was struggling out of bed, crying, 'Let me go, let me go before it's too late . . .!' Goodness knows what the children had written on *her* chart!

In the middle of the ward was a hip-bath full of squashed grapes; and Louisa and Sarah were pretending to be fast asleep with purple feet sticking out from under their blankets . . .

Matron took one long look – at Mrs Bloggs, spinning, at Miss Fizzle studying her chart with a face as flat and white as a pancake, at the stout old lady heaving herself out of bed and streaking down the ward in her red flannel nightie, crying, 'Let me out, let me out!' – at the two pairs of purple feet and the hip-bath . . .

And she turned and looked into the second ward.

Chapter 3

WHILE Staff Nurse was busy in the Women's Ward, this is what the children had been doing in the Men's.

Daniel had altered the patients' charts in there too.

Matthew had changed round the little bed-side lockers where the patients kept their private possessions.

Flavia had tied the cords of their dressing-gowns to the ends of their beds

And Hannah and Joel had got in under the blankets of one of the spare beds and were heaving up and down giving the effect of a very terrible bright red monster . . .

All the other children had done dreadful things too.

Matron stood in the doorway.

Things in here were almost worse than in the

Women's Ward. Several old gentlemen were in full flight, trying to get out of hospital because of the awful things Danny had written on their charts. But as they struggled into their dressing-gowns, they found them suddenly much too large or much too small, and they were in a terrible taking because they thought they had contracted some dread disease which made them shrink – or swell up – all in a minute. And they foraged in their lockers for their slippers and the ones with too-tight dressing-gowns found that their slippers were too big and the ones with their dressing-gowns too big found that their slippers were much too tight; so they thought that all the rest of them had swelled and their feet had shrunk, or the other way about. 'Ow! Ow!' they cried, jostling each other to escape, convinced that they would shrink right down into pygmies (with huge feet) or swell right up into giants (with tiny ones) and be exhibited in circuses for the rest of their lives. 'Let us out! Let us out!' But the cords of their dressing-gowns were tied to their beds and now they either found themselves yanked back and in bed again or – if they were (really) rather fat and strong – towing their beds behind them. 'Ow, ow, *ow*!' cried these ones, even louder, at finding that their beds seemed to be following them about where ever they went, longing to gobble them back in again; and 'Ow, *ow*, OW!' they cried when they saw the Monster bed, with Hannah and Daniel threshing about underneath the red blankets, uttering the huge, hungry growls of a dragon intent upon its prey. Vicky and Tim were kindly dashing about amongst the rest of the patients with basins in case they wanted to be sick. The patients hadn't had the smallest desire to be sick but the sight of the basins made them feel horribly queasy and they joined in the general moaning and groaning and cries of ow, ow, ow!

In the third ward, the upside-down cots had settled into quite a realistic zoo and the Littlest Ones were rampaging up and down behind the

bars, growling and roaring in a very terrible manner and demanding their dinners with a tremendous gnashing of teeth. This greatly alarmed the grown-up patients, who kept poking up scared white faces to see what was happening. Toni, David and Jaci were keeping the animals at bay, banging about with some spare crutches they had found lying around (to the great rage of the one-legged patients, who urgently needed them) and crying: 'Hup! Hup!' and 'Watch that leopard!' and 'They're trying to get at the patients!' and other encouraging remarks. 'The wild beasts have got the children!' cried the patients, seeing the wheels of the cots spinning idly in the air. 'Naughty tiger, let go of that little boy's leg!' cried Toni and Jaci and David immediately, upon hearing this, and 'Now, Leo, one arm will be quite enough for you . . .!' 'After all, they have to be fed,' they said kindly to the patients. 'Oh, dear, when they've finished, they'll start upon us,' cried the one-legged patients, hopping about this way and that, banging into one another and hopping off again. In his corner, stout Podge hid his head under his rice-pudding pillow, bringing it out now and again to take a deep breath and plunge it back once more. He knew that out of all the patients, any lion or tiger in its senses must choose *him* as the fattest and tastiest.

Matron stood in the little central hall. A cot shot past her nose, containing the Baby, swinging happily like a monkey against its bars, crooning a little song, being whizzed back and forth most soothingly along the polished floors, down one ward – a good push from any child that happened to be there – across the hall, down the other ward – a good push from any child that happened to be *there* – and back again.

'Well!' said Matron; and she began to look not at all gentle and saintly and just like Florence Nightingale; but very black and cross indeed. She said to Staff Nurse: 'What is *this*?'

A long train of beds shot past, narrowly missing the Baby in its zooming cot. The children had tied them all together with bandages and were giving the unwilling patients lovely rides, with great ringings of the dinner bell and shoutings of: 'Allstationsto—*Woant*hurt, *Ly*still, *Bee*sick and *Bed*pan . . . All change at *Big*dose, *Little*pill and Wantergotterthe*loo* . . .' Susannah had tied the nurses' apron strings into one big knot and they were struggling furiously in the middle of the ward like a huge, angry octopus, trying to tear itself apart.

Matron looked into the three wards – at Mrs Bloggs circling and buzzing, at Miss Fizzle fuming, at the poor old lady streaking off in her red flannel nightie: at the hip-bath and the purple feet . . . At the old gentlemen scuttling this way and that in their too-tight slippers and their too-big dressing-gowns, towing heaving beds behind them, or being swallowed back in; at the green faces bending over unwanted basins, at the spinning cot wheels and the cages underneath, with their menagerie of Little Ones squealing and growling and gnashing their teeth for their dinners of patients' legs and arms . . . At Podge's round behind stuck up into the air as he crouched with his ostrich head buried under his pillow: at the Baby's cot whizzing innocently back and fore, back and fore – at the octopus of nurses and the train of beds . . . And to the other patients she may still have looked very saintly and gentle and kind, but suddenly, to the children –

Suddenly to the children, she looked – well, she looked like a small, stout, elderly person with a

rusty black dress under her starched white hospital apron, and a bun like a teapot-handle beneath her white nurse's cap; and a nose like two potatoes; and, sticking out over her under-lip, a single, huge big tooth . . .

Nurse Matilda!

'Oh, *lor*'!' said the children; and Nurse Matilda lifted up her big black stick.

Nurse Matilda lifted up her big black stick – and suddenly everything seemed to have changed. Mrs Bloggs was back in her bed again with her poor red face and her high temperature, but happily tucked up and not buzzing a bit. And Miss Fizzle was back in *her* bed, murmuring, 'Temperature normal, home tomorrow,' and as pleased as punch. And all the red flannel nighties were back in *their* beds, not wanting to run away any more; and so were all the old gentlemen in the ward next door. And the Little Ones' cots were the right way up again, and they were all cozed up, fast asleep. And all the other children – well, all the other children were lying back against cool white pillows and nurses were advancing upon them with nice hot drinks . . . It was rather surprising because usually when Nurse Matilda banged with her big black stick, things were not comfortable at all. But still, there they were.

All except Podge Green. Podge still crouched with his head under his pillow, breathing heavily from the cold in his nose and not knowing that the zoo noises had ceased and all was safe again. 'Come dear,' said Staff Nurse going over to him, 'this isn't the way to lie at all. Be a good boy and turn over.' And she gave his striped, round pyjama-bottom a playful smack.

Podge gave one shriek of terror and heaved up in his bed. 'Ow, ow! The adibals have got be! The liods are upod be! I've beed bitted by a tiger, the hippobotobus has bodked be with ids hard, hard hoof, the rhidoscerous has biffed be with ids hard, hard hord . . .'

'Now, now, nonsense!' said Staff Nurse. 'There are no animals here, there never have been, you are perfectly safe. Come, turn over, there's a dear!' Trying to heave him up was a bit like wrestling with a huge, striped boiled pudding, but she got him into a sitting position at last. 'Now, then, dear – lean back!'

All round the wards, the children peered forward, their fists stuffed into their mouths to stop themselves from laughing. Podge gazed resentfully back at them, gave one big, resentful sniff and, exhausted, flopped back against the pillow . . .

'Don't trouble, Staff Nurse. Even if it takes them all night,' said Matron quietly, from her place in the central hall, 'the children will clear up the mess for you.'

You wouldn't have thought that in all the world – let alone in one pillow-case – there could have been so much cold, cloggy, sticky, clinging-to-things, *horrible* rice pudding.

From that day on, the children were so good in

hospital that the nurses, and even Staff Nurse, began to expect little white feathery wings to grow up out of their shoulders any minute. They learnt how to make hospital beds and helped in taking round the meals and cups of tea; and their cheerful shouts of 'Bedpan for Mrs Inagonies!' and 'Quick, quick, he's going to be sick!' would echo down the wards to the great comfort of those in emergency. True, they made some mistakes. Told to give Mrs Chumping an air-ring to sit on, they thought Sister had said 'an airing' and wheeled her out into the garden and raced her round and round in her invalid chair. And when Nurse patted Mr Stout's fat tummy and said he would have to diet, they thought she meant 'dye it' and stripped the struggling old gentleman down and painted him a lively blue. But they were very sorry when they discovered they'd been wrong, and dashed Mrs Chumping back into the ward at the rate of knots (no need to dye *her* blue: she had gone a deep shade of indigo with cold and terror) and stripped Mr Stout down all over again and scrubbed him back to pink. So all in all, a time came when the hospital wondered how it had ever got on without the dear, useful, kindly Brown children; and Nurse Matilda grew less and less ugly every day until she became quite pretty; and then she got prettier and prettier . . .

And then . . .

And then one day Mr and Mrs Brown arrived to see their dear, darling children and their dear, darling children seemed to have got over all their illnesses and operations but they were also getting over being quite so good and Nurse Matilda, I'm afraid, was beginning to look rather more like her old self: very black and cross with her big tooth sticking out in front and her bun of hair sticking out at the back like a teapot-handle; and her nose like two potatoes. 'I think,' she said to Mr and Mrs Brown, 'that it is time the children Had a Change.'

'They could go and stay with their Great-Aunt Adelaide Stitch,' said Mrs Brown. 'She has taken rooms at a seaside hotel with Evangeline and Miss Prawn. I'm sure they'd love to have the children.' The hospital would be sorry to see them go, she added: I told you that she really was rather foolish about her dear, darling children. But still she wasn't quite as foolish as all *that*. 'Perhaps it would be safest if you were to go with them,' she said to Nurse Matilda.

Most children have one fearsome aunt and the Browns had this truly fearsome great-aunt, Great-Aunt Adelaide Stitch. She was very gaunt and tall, with an angry little eye like the eye of a rhinoceros, and her nose was like a rhinoceros horn, only turned upside-down. She was extremely short sighted, which the children often found convenient; and very hard of hearing – she used a large ear trumpet rather like a one-horned cow. She had long ago adopted a little girl called Evangeline who, from being quite a nice, cheerful little lump, had turned into a very stout little, horrid little prig; but fortunately, just what Great-Aunt Adelaide liked. Evangeline had a poor, sad governess called Miss Prawn who, summer and winter alike, suffered quite dreadfully from chilblains on her hands; and a simply horrible pug, which with great imagination was called Pug. The children did not want to go and stay with Great-Aunt Adelaide and Evangeline and Pug and Miss Prawn one bit; but still, it was the seaside and much better than the time they had had to stay with them in town. In fact now that they thought of it, the seaside might be quite fun; and as a matter of fact, the town holiday had been quite fun too – for the children, if not for Great-Aunt Adelaide and Evangeline and Pug and Miss Prawn.

So they said goodbye to Staff Nurse and all the other nurses and the patients and prepared to go. Matron seemed to have disappeared; but Nurse Matilda was all ready in her black button boots and rusty black jacket and rusty black bonnet all trimmed with trembly black jet. Outside the hospital stood a line of cabs called 'growlers' with rather weary looking horses, waiting to take them to the station.

'We can't all fit into those cabs,' said the children. 'The horses are too tired.'

'Nonsense,' said all the grown-ups. 'Get in at once.'

'Oh, dear!' said the children, patting the horses' necks and kissing their soft, pink, velvety noses with their tickley whiskers. 'We're sorry. But what can we do?'

'Whrrrrrrr!' said the horses, blowing back softly into their faces.

'Good idea!' said the children; and when the time came, piled obediently into the cabs.

But the good idea had been to take the floor-boards out of the cabs; so all the children's feet went right through and they ran along gaily (only squashed into rather tight bundles) behind the horses and really were no weight at all. The baby, whose fat little feet wouldn't reach the ground, got carried along, held up by the crush of children in the cab; its short legs whizzing round and round like the wheels of a clockwork engine picked up off the rails.

How Nurse Matilda managed, I'm not quite sure.

Chapter 4

THE station was very exciting, so huge and dim and noisy, with great clouds of steam blowing from the funnels of the engines and a lovely country smell of stables – all the heavy bales and parcels for the goods trains were brought by horse and cart and their stables were lined along the edge of the station. Almond and Agatha almost got left behind, they were so happy talking to the horses; but Nurse Matilda gathered them all together in the end and they filed into the carriages, packed tight together and swinging their feet, delighted to be going off to the seaside at last. The train seemed a bit less delighted; it gave a frightful shriek, as though at the idea of quite so many passengers at one time, and blew off a great deal of steam and a shower of sparks; but the guard wouldn't have any nonsense and waved his green flag in a commanding manner and it began to back out of the station and at last to gather speed, clackety-clack, clackety-clack, clackety-clack – rushing through the country side – dashing into tunnels, screaming at the dark – coming out again into the day-light, on and on and on. Showers of smut and sparks flew out of its funnels and soon the children's faces were covered with little specks like black measles, which made agreeable smudges if you rubbed them with your fingers, especially on each others' faces. By the time they emerged at Puddleton-on-Sea, they certainly were rather a curious sight.

Evening had come by then and it was too dark to see anything but the long line of lights strung out like a necklace of bright beads along the esplanade. But there was a delicious smell of seaweed and the soft sound of the shush-shush-shushing of the waves chasing one another up the sand, and the hiss as they turned round and chased each other back again.

The children filed up at the station in an eager crocodile and marched the short distance to Great-Aunt Adelaide's hotel. This was very large and splendid, with lots of little towers and balconies and squirligigs like a gigantic cuckoo clock. Each child carried its possessions in a basketwork suit case. They were dressed in their white sailor suits (skirts for the girls) and round white sailor hats and I must say they looked extraordinarily silly; but these were their everyday summer clothes and there it was! Still, the sailor suits were complete with whistles on black cords, worn round their necks coming out from their big, square collars; and they thought that something could probably be made out of that. The Baby followed at the end of the crocodile, a bit weary after the long journey but stumping along gamely, its nappies coming down as usual. It had its whistle in its mouth and couldn't get it out because both its fat hands were occupied in lugging along its own little basket; and it certainly breathed rather curiously as it went.

Miss Prawn was on the steps of the hotel, holding out the chilblains in greeting, and Evangeline and Pug bouncing up and down with joy at sight of the army advancing out of the dark. I'm afraid the joy was not very sincere; as you know, the Brown children had stayed with Evangeline before. Sugar and Spice, the dachshunds, upon seeing Pug, ran up and nipped him smartly in the behind. Pug set up a shrill wow-wow-wowing, Evangeline threw herself with loud boo-hoos upon her dear Prawnie, Miss Prawn already was giving small, piercing cries of

despair at the realisation that the Brown children hadn't changed one bit – and now were here for the whole holiday. The children put their whistles to their lips and, blowing away merrily to conceal the uproar from Great-Aunt Adelaide, filed with pious faces into the hall. From the various hotel lounges appeared large, red, white-whiskered colonel-faces and large, angry old-lady-faces, in a state of considerable alarm. Great-Aunt Adelaide proceeded majestically down the stairs towards the children.

At sight of her, they hastily concealed their whistles in their mouths. 'How do you do, children,' said Aunt Adelaide with a stately bow; raising her lorgnette, however, to look with some anxiety into their faces which looked strangely puffed out (by the whistles) and, moreover, as though they had just passed through a black snowstorm. The children tried to reply, but all they could manage (on account of the whistles) was 'Whee-whee-whee-*wheeeeee*,' with a great deal of giggling. Nurse Matilda observed the giggling and banged quietly on the floor with her big black stick.

'You are tired and hungry,' said Aunt Adelaide, peering even more keenly into their train-smudged faces. 'You need a good supper and then up to bed. Chef has prepared a special meal for you.'

'Thick soup, steak and kidney puddings and plum duff,' said Miss Prawn, hopefully. I'm sorry to say that what she was hopeful about was that the children would all develop severe indigestion and spend the rest of the holiday in bed.

'How lovely!' the children tried to say; it was almost their favourite meal. But Nurse Matilda had banged with her big black stick and now the whistles were firmly stuck. 'Whee-*whee*-wheeee!' was all that came out, as they cast longing looks towards the big dining-room.

'Good heavens!' cried Aunt Adelaide, putting up the ear-trumpet. 'The journey has been too much for them altogether!' Even she could get the shrill whistling. 'Acute bronchitis. Up to bed with them immediately! Bread and milk,' she suggested to Nurse Matilda, imperiously, 'and plenty of any medicine you happen to have with you.' She shepherded Evangeline towards the dining-room door. 'Come, my dear, you will have to help eat up as much as possible of the treats prepared for the children. Three helpings of plum duff for *you*!' She looked over Evangeline, who strongly resembled a plum duff herself in her very dreadful dough-coloured dress with large dark spots. 'You could do with a little fattening up, dear child,' she said.

Whistling shrilly, the children marched sadly up to bed, got undressed, climbed in, sat up straight against the rather hard hotel pillows. 'Supper in a minute,' said Nurse Matilda, coming round with a huge bottle of very dreadful looking yellow mixture. 'Doses first. Open your mouths!'

The children shook their heads dumbly. At least you couldn't take doses with your mouth full of whistle. But Nurse Matilda banged once again with her big black stick . . .

After the doses came the bread and milk. Which was worse, it really was quite hard to tell. But when she had tucked them up and gone away for the night, the children said to one another (and they were no longer whistling): 'Didn't you think Nurse Matilda gave a little smile when she said good-night? Didn't you think she really looked – well, quite pretty?'

Except, they had to add, for that terrible sticking-out tooth.

And next morning – the sea! They rushed to the windows and looked out – and there it was: acres and acres of golden sand all washed by the waves, with little foamings of white at the edge of the water as though it hadn't quite got rid of the soap. And between the hotel and the sand, the broad esplanade with the bath-chair men already toiling off on their way to pick up their invalid old ladies and gentlemen and take them for rides along the promenade, like huge, disgruntled babies, sitting up in their prams. On the beach, the Punch and Judy man was putting up his striped canvas upright tent, with its high wooden ledge for Punch and Judy to fight on; the donkeys getting their grooming before the day's work began, giving children rides up and down the beach; a stout brown horse pulling the bathing machines down to the sea's edge so that respectable ladies could change inside and creep down the steps right into deep water, without any gentleman catching a glimpse of them in their bathing dresses – though the bathing dresses were made of good, thick material and came right up to their necks and right down to their ankles.

The children, as soon as breakfast was over, put on their own bathing dresses – which were very high and very long too, but covered with cheerful black and yellow stripes – and looking like a

horde of happy wasps, rushed down across the sand and plunged into the water. Oh, how lovely and rolly and splashy and salty and tumbley that water felt! It bore them up as they floated, frantically paddling with their front paws like little dogs, it tumbled them head-over-heels back to the shore, and sucked away the sand from under them when they tried to stand up, tumbling them back in again. The Baby had got a strand of seaweed around its neck and was curled up into a little round ball, tossing blissfully from ripple to ripple, with its brown, shiny ribbons streaming out behind it. I think it was the happiest hour they had ever had in their lives. Healthy and hearty, they trooped back to the hotel, and fortunately Evangeline hadn't been able to eat up all the steak-and-kidney pudding and plum duff, so Chef had heated up the rest for their lunch. Really, said the children among themselves, they could have a wonderful time here without even ever having to be naughty.

But I'm sure you will be sorry to hear that they *were* naughty; and the very next day. I suppose they had got into the habit of it and simply couldn't stop.

It was a lovely day, fair and unclouded and the sea very still. The children got up early and, in their wasp-bathing-dresses, crept down across the sands and into the water, went out as far as they could and, forming up into a long line, the baby bobbing at the end of it, swam up and down humping up their behinds and making a great deal of splashing. Soon all the elderly inhabitants of Puddleton were out on their balconies in their dressing-gowns, in a great state of excitement at seeing a black-and-yellow striped sea-monster of enormous length, lashing the waters in its rage and obviously looking about it for human prey. A message was sent to the coastguards who in turn sent messages to all the neighbouring seaside places, and soon vast crowds were advancing upon Puddleton-on-Sea. There was a dreadful row in the lifeboat station, little men, quite swallowed up in yellow macintoshes right up to their noses and yellow sou'westers right down to their chins, declaring in muffled voices that wrecks was one thing but dang them! if sea-monsters wasn't another. A great argument blew up, much complicated by the fact that owing to the high collars of the macintoshes and low brims of the sou'westers, no one could hear what anyone else was saying. By the time they had it all sorted out, the sea-monster had broken up into lots of boys and girls running about the beach, wrapped in towels to cover the black and yellow stripes. Clemency and Helen rushed up to the lifeboat men. 'One of our number is missing,' they cried, putting on very long, anxious faces; and added, 'The fattest.'

'Got by that theer monster!' cried the lifeboat men, going very pale.

'Dragged her down to the bottom of the sea,' suggested Nicholas. He explained: 'They bob up and down several times with their victims in their mouths, before they gobble them up.'

'You could drag her out of its jaws next time it comes bobbing up,' suggested Megan helpfully.

'Ow, dang!' said the lifeboat men, not at all charmed by this prospect. They looked round them for inspiration. 'Perhaps she just be 'oiding be' oind they rocks?'

'She couldn't,' said William. 'She couldn't find one large enough.' All the children began to run about, nevertheless, looking under heaps of stacked deck chairs, under the pier, round the bathing machines, earnestly looking for Evangeline, and bringing the lifeboat men's poor hearts still further down into their huge yellow boots with shrill cries of, 'No, she's not here! The monster must have got her! She'll have to be rescued!' And it was quite true that Evangeline was not there; she was humped up sound asleep in her warm hotel bed, making little snortling, snoring noises and one way and another not at all unlike a monster herself.

Nurse Matilda came down the hotel steps and

stood looking out at the beach. She saw the children running about the sands uttering cries of hideous foreboding, she saw the lifeboat men gloomily taking their boat down to the water's edge. They were carrying it upside down so that it looked like a large white beetle with lots of little yellow legs wavering about under it, bent at the knees and very much out of step; muffled cries of, 'Ow, dang!' echoed across the sand as, blinded by its depth, they banged and barged into obstacles which Justin and Louisa were busily putting in their way. Nurse Matilda lifted up her big black stick.

Half the children found themselves in the boat, squashed up between the lifeboat men and uttering a great many ow-dang's! of their own now, as each wave lifted the boat and rolled her this way and that and they all felt more and more sick. The lifeboat men had suddenly become very brave and kept shouting 'Dar she be!' and 'Monster a-hoy!' and rowing off in all directions, only pausing to cry, 'Lean over the side, young master, there, that's roight!' The children tried to explain that there had been no sea-monster really but they seemed to feel too sick to utter; and now lifeboats began appearing from all the other stations and soon there was a positive little regatta of them, and the water echoed with cries of 'Dang!' and 'Dar she blows!' and 'She'll be 'oiding in that there rough water over there, make for the

breakers!' The children leaned over the side and, silently heaving, longed for the shore . . .

But ashore, the rest of them were still searching. They searched and they searched. They knew that Evangeline wasn't lost, but Nurse Matilda had banged with her big black stick, and they had to go on looking for her. The heaps of stacked deck chairs nipped their fingers, the sharp rocks scratched their bare toes, the tall metal struts under the pier were slimy with seaweed, the waves came whishing in and swept their feet from under them so that they sat down abruptly in pools of chilly water – but they had to go on clambering about, idiotically calling out for Evangeline. Miss Prawn came out on to the esplanade and ran up and down with plaintive bleats of terror, her chilblains clasped to her flat bosom. Pug followed her faithfully and Sugar and Spice faithfully followed Pug. 'Wow, dang!' yapped Pug, as nip-nip went Sugar and Spice at his behind; or at any rate, it sounded very much like it. The children toiled on.

The Baby toiled with them. Up and down the beach it tottered, its nappies coming down as usual, its little pink starfish hands held out anxiously before it, cries of 'Egangekeeng!' and 'Cay peag!' rending the air. 'Oh, yes,' said the children; and, 'Please!' they all begged Nurse Matilda, standing round her in an imploring circle; but for once even this magic word made no difference and on and on they went . . .

In her hotel bedroom, Evangeline heard the cries in her sleep and, like some monster indeed, stirring in the deeps, humphed herself out of bed, put on one of her very ghastly dresses, of purple with crimson blotches, most suitable for a sunny day at the sea, stumped downstairs to join dear Prawnie for some Healthful Fresh Air before breakfast. So dense was the crowd on the esplanade, hoping like anything to see the monster coming up, dripping, with a fat little girl in its mouth, that even Evangeline in the dress escaped notice; and hearing a small, piping cry of 'Egangekeeng!' she stepped up to the Baby and said, innocently: 'Yes?'

'Egangekeeng!' cried the Baby and jumped so hard for joy that its nappies really did come right down and lay in a round white nest, with its fat little feet in the middle like two pink eggs. It hauled the nappies up hastily, blushing a little all over its sweet, round face and, holding the nappies up with one hand, tugged Evangeline with the other to Nurse Matilda. 'I koung Egangekeeng, I koung Egangekeeng!' it cried, joyfully presenting its prize who stood like a stout purple cow, staring stupidly at the commotion around her. The children all came and gathered about them. 'So, Nurse Matilda, can we stop searching now?'

'Certainly not,' said Nurse Matilda. 'You have given a great deal of trouble, severely frightened a good many people and spoilt a lovely sunny morning for everyone. You had better go on as you chose to begin.'

This was dreadful. They saw themselves spending the whole of the rest of their holiday – the whole of the rest of their *lives* – beach-combing for Evangeline; looking more and more curious as they got older and older, so that at last no one would have anything to do with them and they must live on limpets and seaweed, curled up at nights beneath the dank pier, in their black and yellow bathing dresses like a little swarm of sodden bees. They cried out piteously: 'Oh, Nurse Ma*til*da—!'

The baby looked up into her face and its big blue eyes filled with tears. 'But I *koung* her,' it protested.

'Oh, Nurse Matilda,' said the children. 'The poor Baby! It's so proud of having found her. At least let the Baby stop!'

Nurse Matilda stooped down and picked up the Baby and held it warm and safe against her shoulder. 'Ah!' she said. 'That's the first thing you've done today that hasn't been selfish and unkind.' And just for a moment, there came round her, her little golden glow: and in that one moment the seas were empty, the crowds had gone and the Brown family was sitting down comfortably to breakfast.

But up at the lifeboat station, the little yellow men, dressed up in their tarpaulins and sou'-westers, all ready for a wreck, were shaking their heads in amazement . . . 'Dang me if Oi didn't have a strange dream laast noight,' they were saying to one another . . .

Chapter 5

THAT day, after lunch, the children were sent off for a walk. 'I have allowed Miss Prawn to bring her mother with her for the holiday,' said Aunt Adelaide. 'You can all take turns in pushing her along the promenade, in her bath-chair.' Miss Prawn's mother was a very dreadful old lady. She had once had a deep passion for cheese but the children had sent her a bar of soap instead and now she much preferred that and as a result was in a constant state of lather. As she had just had a substantial meal, her bath-chair soon became almost invisible in clouds of foam. The Baby, stumping along in the rear of the crocodile, kept getting swept into it, disappearing from sight for a while and emerging, all smiles, with its nappies coming down as usual.

Other old ladies and gentlemen stopped to stare. 'Beaten white of egg,' explained the children. 'A new treatment. Takes years off your age!' The old ladies and gentlemen set up a great hullabalooing because *they* couldn't be covered in beaten white of egg too. Their bath-chair men gathered round them in heated argument, Miss Prawn joined them full of anxious denials. The children, while her back was turned, quickly swapped two bath-chairs and they set off once more; now wheeling a stout gentleman, very happy in the belief that he had suddenly been covered in white of egg and would emerge from the foam practically a schoolboy again. In fact he emerged still a stout old man, covered up in rugs – to the dreadful dismay of Miss Prawn who thought the whole thing had been too much for her mother, who had suddenly blown up very big and red, and grown a large white moustache. The children proceeded meekly on their way. They had found a live jelly-fish and contrived to place it on top of Evangeline's head, where it lay very dank and quivery, its tentacles constantly falling over her eyes and being brushed aside with loud appeals to Prawnie because her hair seemed to have got all wet. Miss Prawn, however, had decided that the moustache must just be soap-suds and was trying to scrape it off, to the great rage of the old gentleman – even her Mama's voice appeared to have taken a turn for the worse; and for once she was deaf to Evangeline's appeals. 'Oh, Evangeline, it's not only your hair, the whole top of your head seems to have gone all soft!' cried the children, helpfully. Evangeline

put up her hand, felt only cold, wet jelly and bolted for home. Pug followed her, yapping at her heels, and Sugar and Spice followed close behind him, nipping away.

The children marched serenely on, pausing only for Camilla and Jocelyn to give a slight twist to the sign at the crossroads, which said on one arm TO LITTLE PIDDLINGTON and on the other TO PUDDLETON-ON-SEA. On the way back, they passed a large nursing home where a desperate scene was in progress because the bath-chair man who had wheeled away a stout, red-faced old gentleman with a large white moustache, had returned with a thin, pale old lady, loudly demanding tea and a bar of Sunlight Soap. The Browns took no notice but filed innocently by. At Ocean View and Sandybanks and the Bay Hotel, landladies were having heated arguments with total strangers who, thanks to the sign-post, were under the impression that they had safely arrived in Little Piddlington, and now, declaring that they had booked rooms in advance, were angrily forcing their way in, children, luggage, dogs and all. No doubt in the real Little Piddlington, scenes of the same nature were going on. Ocean View and Sandybanks being next door to one another, Danny and Joel were able, while the people were indoors quarrelling, to mix up all the luggage so that nobody knew whose was whose, and there soon followed a tremendous uproar, sorting that out too. Farther down the road, Hilary and

Quentin had unscrewed the sign from a gate saying, in ornamental letters, HAPPY-HOLME BOARDING HOUSE and exchanged it with the one next door saying LIBERTY HALL, which, as the guests were to discover, was not the same thing at *all*.

The junior boys of a local school filed by in a crocodile of pairs, following their master, all dressed (except for the master, who I must say would have looked even sillier) in the regulation white summer sailor suits. The younger boys of the Brown family, similarly attired, immediately attached themselves to the end of the queue and marched along with them, throwing their arms back and forth with a martial swing, heads held high – to the great bewilderment of the master who, having started out with a dozen boys, now found himself with about thirty. 'Spots before the eyes,' he kept saying to himself, counting the boys over and over again. 'It was that lobster for lunch.' The boys seemed badly out of step and he cried out, 'Left – *right*! Left – *right*!' in a sergeant-major voice. The boys from the school did a little skip to get back into step and the Browns at once did a little skip to get them out again. At the entrance to their hotel, they peeled silently off from the end of the crocodile, leaving the master more mystified than ever. 'Spots before the eyes is one thing,' he wrote earnestly home to his mother that evening, 'but boys before the eyes is another. And this morning, I thought I saw more boys than were really there. I shan't eat lobster again.' And poor man – he did love it! It was rather a shame.

The children went quietly into the dining-room and sat down in fours and sixes at the little hotel tables. The old ladies and gentlemen looked tenderly into their innocent, radiant faces and said to each other that it was pleasant to have the place enlivened by a little sprinkling of Youth. The sprinkling was in fact rather a heavy shower but they hadn't come to realise that yet; and they watched with enthusiasm the way the children, who appeared to have rescued a large and quivering jelly-fish from some situation of peril, carried it lovingly down to the sea and set it free.

Between tea time and supper the children were very busy:

Francesca and Teresa had let out the seams of some of Evangeline's dresses and taken in the seams of some of the others; and Aunt Adelaide and Miss Prawn were in a terrible taking because the poor child seemed to be changing so rapidly from fat to thin.

Matthew had put fruit salts in the sugar sifter and everybody's pudding was beginning to fizzle, and –

Lucy had written with a soft pencil on top of the bald patch of the head waiter YOU ARE ALL SILLY OLD FOOLS; *and every time he turned his back on anyone, they rose up in great wrath and gave notice.*

All the other children were doing simply dreadful things too.

And so the days went sunnily by. The skies were as blue as the sea and the sea was as blue as the sky and all glittery with dancing points of light. The sand was golden and smooth, with only some hard, damp wrinkles where the tide had turned and gone out again. Along the water's edge stood the bathing machines all day, in a long row. They were like little gypsy caravans and each morning a stout brown horse with wet brown legs, towed them down into the water, led by a stout old woman with wet *red* legs, who unharnessed him there and took him back for another one. The ladies from the hotels hurried

across the beach in their nice, dark serge summer dresses with their large hats and parasols, climbed up the steps and dived behind a thick curtain, each into her own little caravan; and, clad in a dark serge bathing dress which began at her neck and ended in long frilled drawers down to her ankles, her head covered in a huge frilled cap, crept coyly down the steps on the side that led into the water. The bathing machines, as we know, were pulled in so far, that the water was deep enough to cover them up to their necks the moment they got into it: so that nothing so dreadful could happen as a gentleman catching even a glimpse of the long serge drawers. In the water they bobbed up and down, often holding on for safety to the lady with the wet red legs, and uttering shrill screams of what the children supposed must be delight, before hurrying up the steps into their caravans again.

The children had a splendid time diving in under the machines and banging smartly on the underneaths of their floors (so that the poor ladies thought there might be gentlemen hiding there spying upon the moment when they should descend into the sea): or tugging away at the wheels pushing the bathing machines higher up the beach, so that the bathers had to come right up out of the water to climb back in: goodness, if a gentlemen had seen them *then*! (Actually, the gentlemen were quite safe, on a decently distant part of the beach, also covered from head to foot in solid bathing dresses, mostly striped, splashing about in manly fashion, and dashing modestly back across the sand to change behind the rocks. The children contented themselves with switching the little heaps of clothes left beneath the various rocks, so that there was a fine old scrummage, stout elderly parties trying to struggle into bright club blazers many sizes too small for them, smart young blades clapping on straw hats and finding themselves suddenly blind and deaf.)

The little donkeys chiff-chuffed through the sand giving children rides, and the Brown children spent all their pocket-money buying rides and not having them, so that the donkeys could rest. They got Pug into a frill and put him up on the ledge of the Punch and Judy booth, to the great rage of Pug and alarm of the Punch and Judy man, who thought his Toby had suddenly had his long, thin terrier nose flattened in; and to the great delight of the real Toby who had a splendid time, running about playing with Sugar and Spice – rushing into the sea and rushing straight out again to shake themselves all over whoever happened to be near them. I must confess that Sugar and Spice were not the most popular dogs on the beach, that sunny summer at Puddleton-on-Sea.

And I'm afraid the Browns weren't the most popular children.

Chapter 6

AND so, as I say, the days passed; till one afternoon Great-Aunt Adelaide announced that she would give a picnic party on the beach.

Great-Aunt Adelaide's idea of a picnic was to arrange a large ring of deck chairs on the sand, as close to the hotel as possible, and invite all the more old and ferocious ladies of the hotel as her guests; with her own maid, Fiddle, to wait upon the company. The children spent a busy morning in preparation for this treat, and this is what they were doing:

Sally and Adam were gluing together the wooden struts of one of the deck chairs.

Cecily and Roland were making small slits across the seats.

Marcus and Camilla were boring three narrow passages through the sand, leading to the middle of where the tablecloth would be spread; and starting off a crab at each entrance.

Felicity and Lucy were collecting bits of foam from the sea and forming it into little balls which really did make the most life-like meringues.

Almond and Theodora were lining the sand-wiches with seaweed.

Mary was filling up the sugar bowls with nice, white sand, and—

Sarah Jane and Alexander had borrowed a performing seal from the aquarium (without asking the keeper's permission) and seated him, wrapped in a rug from the waist downward, in one of the deck chairs; and painted a white collar round his neck.

All the other children were doing simply dreadful things too.

The ladies assembled in stout cloth dresses with stout linen petticoats over several stout *flannel* petticoats, and wearing large hats covered with feathers and flowers – evidently their idea of comfortable wear for a boiling hot day at the seaside. Evangeline was adorned in one of her more hideous garments, mustard yellow splodged quite horribly with a sickly green; with a floppy hat which fell down all round her fat red face, most mercifully concealing it from the beholders. Fiddle hovered anxiously outside the circle, waiting to hand cups and plates. The children had filled her shoes with the real meringues and little clouds of white puffed up round her ankles with every step; the cream had sunk down to the bottom and made a very satisfying squlidge, squlidge as she trudged wretchedly about in the sand.

The ladies assembled with joyful cries of admiration at the feast laid out on the white tablecloth at their feet. One sponge cake was missing, which Rhiannon had thoughtfully removed in advance and was now quietly crumbling on top of the large flowered hats. There was a fearful struggle with Miss Prawn's deck chair, which refused to open. Evangeline rushed to her dear Prawnie's assistance and they emerged at last, their hands full of broken wood, wrapped in the red and white striped canvas, like two pale prunes in a slice of streaky bacon. The rest of the guests were settling down happily, all unaware that beneath them the little slits in the canvas were beginning slowly to get larger. 'But who is the very dark gentleman with the moustaches?' they murmured admiringly to Great-Aunt Adelaide. 'Pray present us!'

The dark gentleman presented himself, in a growly voice which appeared to come from very deep down – almost from underneath his deck chair, one might have said. 'Reverend George Tomlinson-Seal, dear ladies,' he replied. 'Retired missionary from Mmmmm–glummmba-Mmmmmglummmba. You will pardon my not rising to salute you. I have unfortunately lost my legs.'

'What, both of them?' cried the ladies, perturbed; and it did sound rather careless.

'Sacrifice to my parishioners,' said the reverend gentleman. 'My dear Mmmmm-glummmba-Mmmmmglummmbans.' A very special feast, he explained. One could hardly offer less.

'A feast?' cried the ladies, growing rather pale.

'Ah, well, one was younger then. I daresay,' said the Reverend, with jocular modesty, 'that I'd prove a rather tougher dish nowadays!'

'*Dish?*'

'Cannibals to a man, dear fellows!' From beneath the deck chair came a loud smacking of lips. 'And one really couldn't blame them. A nice plump young girl, for example – one does get a taste for it.' He looked round the laden tablecloth. 'Those sandwiches – not by any chance –?'

'Fiddle!' said Aunt Adelaide, sharply commanding. Fiddle, lint white in the face, squlidged through the sand with the plate, snatching back her arm in great haste as the guest reached out for a sandwich. With one large hand which, despite the heat of the day, appeared to be clad in a rather damp dark fur glove, he picked one up and thrust it, whole, into his mouth. 'Only strawberry jam,' said the growly voice, disappointed. 'I had for a moment hoped . . . And I *prefer* it raw . . .' The faint squeals of the ladies prevented any further confessions. He rose rather rockily to his feet. 'I had better get back to my lodgings. They understand my requirements there. Perhaps one or two of these dear children would come with me?' He looked rather longingly at the stout figure of Evangeline.

Miss Prawn flung herself in front of Evangeline with outspread arms, ready to defend her to the last crumb. Sarah Jane and Alexander each took a flipper – I mean an arm – of the unwelcome guest and, still wrapped in the rug, he unsteadily departed.

The keeper was much surprised to see one of his seals being supported back into the aquarium by two kind children with innocent looks on their faces. He now wore no rug but appeared to have a white band painted round his neck, and to

have been eating strawberry jam. 'You never know what these varmints'll get up to,' said the keeper, giving the seal a playful shove to get it back into the pool and reaching for a bucket of fish. Unfortunately he was somewhat short of sight and Sarah Jane and Alexander had to catch most of the fish and pass it on, the seal applauding with a great clapping of flippers, licking his lips at the delicious mixture of raw fish and strawberry jam. The children wiped the fish off their hands down the sides of their clothes and went back to the picnic party. 'Goodness,' they cried, 'you should see his landlady's children!' Not one of them still complete, they said, with all its limbs; but no-body seemed to mind a bit, they were all delighted to give an arm here, a leg there, to keep Mr. Tomlinson-Seal happy and at home, so far from his dear Mmmmm–glummmba-Mmmmm-glummmbans. And indeed you could see how glad he was to be back with the family; he was evidently devoted to children. 'He loved *you*,' they said, meaningfully to Evangeline; and added, in great consternation: 'Why has Miss Prawn fainted away? He only likes *fat* people.'

The ladies had not been having the happiest of times. When they took sips of tea, the sand-sugar filled their mouths uncomfortably with grit; after Mr Seal's visit they no longer cared much for red jam sandwiches and jelly, and when they reached for a lovely fluffy white meringue, it was only sea-foam and their teeth met the middle with a jolting click. If they had any left, that is; for the seaweed sandwiches had proved the greatest success of all, the ladies' teeth becoming clamped on the seaweed and coming away with it: so that they sat chumbling angrily on their poor gums, while their teeth remained, grinning back at them rather dreadfully, fixed into the sandwiches in their hands. And when they might have turned to a nice, soft, chumbley sponge cake – the sponge cake seemed to have disappeared . . .

The sponge cake, as we know, had been crumbled by Rhiannon into the crowns of the ladies' large hats.

It was a beautiful day. In the golden dazzle of the sunshine, the sky was all hazily blue, the sea sparkled as though it had been sprinkled with diamonds, its white fingers tickling their way up the beach and hastily scuttling back, with a little sighing sound, as though it were playing a game, trying to see how far it could creep up to the people's bare toes before anyone noticed it . . . All around them were other picnic parties, children with buckets and spades, children playing cricket, children paddling at the water's edge, holding the hands of mothers and fathers with bunched-up skirts and rolled-up trouser legs. Heads bobbed in the water, nannies were drying their charges, wrapped up in enormous striped beach towels, rubbing away so vigorously that the poor little heads rolled helplessly, hair flopping, on the slender necks. Whole families were earnestly building sand-castles, tunnelling tiny arches and door-ways which collapsed slowly inwards as the damp sand dried out in the sun. Above it all, the seagulls called shrilly, wheeling, drifting, suddenly swooping down . . .

It wasn't long before their beady eyes spotted the bits of cake which Rhiannon had dropped into the ladies' hats.

The ladies, being friends of Great-Aunt Adelaide, were, as we've said, mostly very large and rather fierce. There was an angry, stout old party called Mrs Grobble and another very angry stout old party called Mrs Rumbletum and a simply furious stout old party with a strong foreign accent, called Mrs Guttziz; and there was also poor Miss Fizzle who had come down here to convalesce. You remember Miss Fizzle? – the children had changed over the charts at the hospital and her temperature seemed to have shot up suddenly from normal to a hundred and four. She had never quite got over it and now she went quite pale when a seagull dived down and seized a bit of cake from the crown of her hat. 'Eaouw! Eaouw!' cried Miss Fizzle in ladylike accents, and 'Ow, ow!' cried all the other ladies and 'Owchn, Owchn!' cried Mrs Guttziz as peck, peck, peck went the hard beaks banging away for crumbs, at the tops of their heads.

But soon the last morsel was gone and there came little tearing sounds, as bits of ribbon and

feather and lace began to go too, not to mention large lumps of imitation flowers and fruit, from the hats themselves; and at last – a whole hat. 'Oh, Mrs Grobble, look at your bald head!' cried the children, helpfully, and, 'Ow, ow, my hat!' cried Mrs Grobble, scarlet in the face with outraged dismay.

'We'll get it for you,' cried the children and off they went. 'A comet, a comet!' they declaimed, dashing about the beach in little doomladen groups. 'A comet descending! The end of the world has come!' The people looked up and saw a bright object sailing above them, with long strands streaming behind it of Mrs Grobble's rich brown hair, and they snatched up their children, spades, buckets and all and made tracks for home. The seagull, disturbed by the fuss, flew out to sea and dropped the hat. 'An octopus! An octopus!' screamed the children, deserting the beach to flock down to the water's edge. 'Swim for it! You'll all be seized and dragged down to the bottom of the sea!' And indeed a very dreadful creature it looked, bright blue and pink, covered with large irregular lumps of what had once been artificial roses, and trailing its rippling tentacles of net and hair. The bathers took one look at it and struck out for the shore.

Back at the picnic, Mrs Grobble sat almost bursting with rage and mortification, looking like a monster Easter egg, crimson in the face right up to her forehead, where the colour suddenly stopped, leaving a bald white dome. The hat was washed gently in to the edge of the beach and the children rescued it and helpfully slapped it back on to her head. They had got it wrong way round and she sat looking very balefully out at them from behind the long strands of dripping wet hair. But after all, they were only being kind to her – weren't they?

Two other seagulls had meanwhile seized Mrs Guttziz's hat and Mrs Rumbletum's but, scared by all the noise, soon dropped them and flew off. Unfortunately the hats fell back on to the wrong heads. Mrs Guttziz peered through her lorgnette at Mrs Rumbletum, who now wore an enormous confection of orange and pink which sat very oddly above her rather purple face. 'Mrs Rumpletoom – I haf not perfore opserfing that we are wearing the same hetz!'

'Why, no indeed,' said Mrs Rumbletum,

recognising her own hat on Mrs Guttziz's head.

'A ferry hendsome het. Extra-ortinary,' said Mrs Guttziz, looking at *her* hat on Mrs Rumbletum's head, 'thet we shoult buyink both the same.' She added with charming frankness that on Mrs Rumbletum's part, it had been a great mistake. 'Your complexion iss not gutt. Qvuite wronk to choosing oranche for colour off a het.'

'My hat is pale blue,' said Mrs Rumbletum, gazing at it as it sat perched on top of Mrs Guttziz.

'Oranche,' said Mrs Guttziz, gazing back at her own hat, on Mrs Rumbletum. She appealed to the other ladies who up to now had been riveted (rather joyfully I'm afraid) upon Mrs Grobble's misadventures, with her own octopus hat. 'What colour would you sayink iss Mrs Rumpletoom's het?'

'Orange,' said the ladies, a trifle astonished at finding Mrs Rumbletum's large purple face now crowned as with fire; but not yet able to collect their wits.

'Oranche,' said Mrs Guttziz, triumphantly. But she peered still more closely through her glasses at Mrs Rumbletum and suddenly let out a loud bellow of alarm. 'Move beck! Be careful! She iss goink out of her mindt!'

'What's the matter?' cried all the ladies, driving the hind feet of their deck chairs deeper and deeper back into the sand, as they tried to move away from the dangerous Mrs Rumbletum.

'The seagulse hes pecked too hardt on her head and this hes affected her mindt. Yellow hair,' said Mrs Guttziz, firmly reminding them. 'From out a bottle, perheps, I am not sayink: but yellow. Ant now – look et it! You are hearink of people goink grey in one night. In fife min'yutes, Mrs Rumpletoom is goink white as snow.' Mrs Guttziz's own hair was as white as snow, but most of it had come away, speared with two large hatpins to her hat, which now, of course, hair and all, sat upon Mrs Rumbletum's head.

Mrs Rumbletum had had an unhappy afternoon. She had been much shaken by the cannibal revelations of the Reverend Tomlinson-Seal, then at finding her gums clashing together as her teeth were carried away, fixed into a seaweed sandwich held in her hand. There were still remnants in her mouth of mixed sand-sugar and sea-foam; and suddenly for a moment she had felt her head go very light and airy, only a moment later to become as though a heavy weight lay upon it. Now all the ladies were staring at her, open-mouthed, assuring her that her pale blue hat was bright orange and her golden hair was white. (It was true that Mrs Rumbletum's gold came out of a bottle; but at least her hair belonged to her head; only now it was covered with Mrs Guttziz's white hair, complete with the orange hat.) She rose to her feet, trembling all over like a great blackcurrant jelly, crowned with gold. 'Yes,' she said simply. 'I am going mad.' And she crossed her wrists dramatically before her, as though ready for the strait-jacket. 'Take me away!'

The children, delighted to do so, clustered round to lead her off as she seemed to be so anxious to go; but suddenly . . .

Suddenly everything seemed to happen at once. The crabs had long ago started down the three little passages which Marcus and Camilla had tunnelled, leading to the middle of the picnic tablecloth. Sugar and Spice and Pug, sniffing happily round, had discovered the entrances and each chosen one and started tunnelling in on his own. Unfortunately, at the end of each, was sitting very contentedly under the tablecloth a large live crab. Nip, nip, nip went the crabs, confronted by three moist black noses; and Wow, wow, wow! went Sugar and Spice and Pug, trying to back away; and 'Ow, ow, ow!' cried the ladies in dreadful alarm as the whole picnic suddenly seemed to come alive. Cups and saucers flew up

in the air and came down with a crash, cakes and sandwiches flung themselves about as though the beach had erupted beneath them, the teapot shot up and streamed hot brown tea, the milk jugs shot up and streamed cold white milk, the foam meringues wafted about like little clouds, the seaweed sandwiches split wide and showed their glossy brown. There was a tremendous ow-ow-owing as the ladies struggled to their feet and fled in a panic stricken rout, streaking out across the sand to the safety of the hotel, led by Great Aunt Adelaide Stitch, fearfully hooting through her high, rhinoceros-horn nose.

Soon the whole beach was in confusion. The stout button-boots of the ladies crashed in mad stampede through the parties of picnickers, games of cricket, circles of aunties and mums, gossiping over their knitting, sitting round on their little striped camp stools, happy though hot. Mrs Grobble had got one foot stuck in a child's tin bucket and made a terrible clanking as she pounded along, Mrs Rumbletum had snatched up a wooden spade and threshed about, clearing her formidable path. Clouds of crushed meringue flew up about Fiddle's lean legs as she squelched through the sand, still clutching a teapot and dreadfully dribbling hot brown tea as she ran. Poor Prawnie, blinded by lather, was madly pushing her mother's bath chair this way and that, zooming up a rock with it, down the other side – feet hardly touching the ground – galloping across sand-castles to the cries of outraged children, driving her wild way slap over the tummies of furious old gentlemen, sleeping on the sand with newspapers spread over their faces . . . Sugar and Spice and Pug had emerged and shaken off their crabs, and now fled about through the confusion, hysterically barking; the crabs scuttled down to the sea again, nipping right, left and centre as they went. Through it all, the children ran crying, 'A volcano! It's erupting! Fly for your lives . . .!' And at last, as the beach emptied and they found themselves alone, collapsed into the deck chairs round the wreck of Great-Aunt Adelaide's picnic, and lay there, speechless with laughter.

Nurse Matilda stood on the edge of the promenade and looked down on them; and lifted up her big black stick . . .

And the little slits in the canvas began to grow. They grew and they grew; and the children slowly sank down and down till their bottoms touched the sand and their knees were tight up under their chins. And there they all stayed.

From the esplanade above them, came the clamour of children screaming for abandoned buckets and spades, of families sorting themselves out from other families – many were so plastered with sand as to be unrecognisable; of nannies giving notice, of hotel guests packing up and departing for ever; or departing for ever, with*out* packing up, in terror of the volcano. But as time went by, the sounds grew less and less and at last silence fell. The hot day cooled, a little breeze came from over the waters, carrying with it the briny scent of the sea; the tide crept in, smoothing out with its white fingers of foam, the poor, torn-up, tumbled sand – and softly crept out again. The sun went down. The evening came.

Curled up tight with their chins on their knees – the children cried out: 'Oh, Nurse Matilda,

please help us! Please let us go!' But all was silent and quiet. No answer came.

And night fell and the moon rose and in its light the sea lay like wrinkled black treacle; and there was no sound but the sh-sh-sh of the waves, murmuring a lullaby to all the living things in the deeps of the ocean.

Murmuring a lullaby . . . The children's eyes stared up, unblinking, at the winking stars. They longed and longed for sleep – but they were wide awake. The sea was singing its lullaby to them but they were caught there, fastened for ever and ever, and could not even go to sleep. They rocked and wriggled in the fast clasp of the wooden arms of the deck chairs. 'If only we could get free!' they said. 'If only we could get free, we'd run away. It's horrible here at the seaside, we could run away and go back to our own dear home . . .' But they couldn't get free; the deck chairs held them tight.

And suddenly a voice said: 'Where's the Baby?' and another voice said, with a shake in it, 'Yes, what's happened to the Baby?' and another voice said with a break in it, 'With all the rushing about and laughing and having fun, we forgot all about the Baby . . .' And another voice said with tears in it: 'We've been selfish, and beastly, making things horrid for other people and spoiling their day; and not even given a thought to our own poor Baby . . .'

And Nurse Matilda stood up there on the promenade with the drowsy baby held safe against her shoulder, and looked down at them and listened: and smiled. And if the children could have seen her face in the moonlight, I think they would have said: 'All of a sudden – doesn't she look *beautiful*?'

If only it hadn't been for that one huge tooth sticking straight out over her lower lip.

Nurse Matilda lifted up her big black stick and brought it down – but very gently. And the tight wooden deck chairs released their hold and the moon drew a veil of cloud across her bright face, so that all was dark and quiet; and the sea sang its murmurous lullaby; and the children's eyes closed – and they were fast asleep.

Fast asleep – and dreaming.

Chapter 7

HE children were dreaming. They dreamed that the deck chairs released their hold; and they all leapt to their feet and cried: 'We'll run away! Let's run away! Let's run home!' And they began to run.

They ran and they ran. The moon had drawn aside her veiling of cloud and shone down brightly on the wrinkled black sea, and the blurred white sand. Along the beach, they went – scattering the ruins of sand-castles, hopping over crumpled tin buckets and broken wooden spades, crashing through abandoned picnics, skipping over deck chairs trampled into match-wood in the panic stampede after the eruption of the volcano beneath their own picnic. They ran and they ran. Hopping over more spades and buckets, more picnics, more smashed-up deck chairs – and more of them and more of them and more . . . The beach seemed very long and when Puddleton-on-Sea was left far behind them, still the sand stretched on ahead. And, it was very awkward, but as they ran, little stinging puffs of crushed white sugar seemed to be rising in clouds about their ankles, and squlidge, squlidge went their feet, sucking in and out of their shoes as though they had been filled with whipped cream. The Big Ones were in the lead, the Middling Ones following, the Little Ones helping the Tinies, trailing behind. In the rear came Pug with his round, pale brown behind and his stump of tail; and nip, nip, nip went Sugar and Spice, following Pug; and nip, nip, nip went three large, angry crabs, following Sugar and Spice. 'Wow wow wow!' went Pug and 'Wow wow wow!' went Sugar and Spice and nip, nip, nip went the crabs; and, 'Oh, dear,' cried the Little Ones, passing it along the line, up to the Middling Ones and so on up to the Big Ones in the lead, 'we're so tired. Can't we stop running, just for a minute?'

But somehow they couldn't stop running. They had to go on.

They ran and they ran. Miss Prawn appeared

from nowhere, belting along beside them, her chilblains glowing rosily through the white foam as she propelled her mother's bath-chair. The old lady sat very contentedly, munching at a bar of soap. It made the children hungry, just to hear her jaws snap on each new bite. 'Couldn't you spare us just a crumb?' they begged. 'But it's soap,' said a disembodied voice from deep within the foam. 'Why must she always eat soap?' cried the children, resentfully, jogging on. 'Well, it *is a bath*-chair,' said Miss Prawn loyally, jogging too.

They ran and they ran. And now all the cream

had gone and their shoes were filled with little icicles and their feet were getting very cold, and yet at the same time their heads were getting very hot and they realised that, his stout form wobbling like a jelly as he went, Podge Green was lollopping along beside them. 'Don't come near us, don't come near us,' cried the children, 'you'll give us your cold!' But they realised that what they really were saying was 'Dote cub dear us, dote cub dear us,' and they'd got it already. Still, that did seem to settle it. 'We're ill,' they cried. 'We've got codes id our doses, we bust go idto hospidal!' And sure enough, up rushed a fleet of little men, bearing stretchers, all at the ready. But just as they were about to stop the children running by sheer force, and strap them on to the stretchers (still feebly kicking, no doubt, but covered with nice red blankets to tuck them in) Sir Minsupp Izgizzard appeared, holding up a commanding hand. 'Women and horses first!' he cried, and up out of the sea came a horde of stout little old women with wet red legs, each leading a stout horse with wet *brown* legs – and the ambulance men set upon *them* instead, and soon had them all comfortably settled on the stretchers. With a ringing of bells and stamping of hooves, a fleet of horse-drawn ambulances came dashing across the sand and, already neighing away in a very showing-off manner about their operations, the stout brown-legged horses were carried off, with the stout red-legged ladies in their wake. The children ran on and now they turned and spun in dizzy little circles as they ran. 'It's too buch,' they cried. 'We've got codes, we're ill, we're dyig, we cad't go od.' But they had to, just the same.

But salvation was in sight; for there ahead of them stood Mr Privy, the Vicar, and surely he must love his neighbours and stop them running if he could. He looked rather odd, his neat suit of clerical grey being crowned by a small black velvet nightcap; but the children were thankful to see him, nightcap and all. They set up a little song, managing as well as they could, considering their colds. 'People who are kide ad beek, Bister Privy,' sang the children, 'Ad always turd the other cheek, Will fill their lives with berry fud, Bister Privy, Ad be belov'd by everywud,' and they jogged up and down, marking time and confidently waiting for Mr Privy to turn the other cheek and become lovable. But Mr Privy only burst into a hymn of his own. 'On-ward Christ-yun so-ho-hol-diers,' sang Mr Privy, and instead of turning his cheek, held out his hand and warmly shook each of theirs as they passed by . . .

And as they passed by again . . . And as they passed by *again* . . . For now the children found themselves running round and round in a circle, shaking hands with Mr Privy, and running on round. And it seemed that this might have gone on for ever, if there had not appeared across the face of the moon a dark veil which resolved itself into a swarm of bees. 'Rud for it, rud for it, Bister Privy!' cried the children, rudding for it thebselves – I mean running for it themselves. 'There's a swarb of bees.' '*I*'b dot frighted of bees,' said Mr Privy (for even he seemed to have caught the infection), and remained where he was with out-stretched hand and a pleasant word ready for each comer. 'But they're dot bees after all,' cried the children. 'Look, look!' – and indeed the bees had all clustered together now, and they saw that the swarm was really a sea-monster, striped yellow and black, which had risen up out of the water and was making for them with a very determined look upon its terrifying face. 'A bodster, bodster!' cried the children running harder than ever; at least not in circles now, however, but streaking out across the sand, led by Mr Privy and with Miss Prawn at full pelt by their side; only her mother sitting chumping away happily, quite safe within her blanket of white. Sugar and Spice and Pug brought up the rear with the three crabs still going nip, nip, nip behind.

Or rather the *two* crabs: for the sea-monster had closed upon them now and reached out a great curled, flaming tongue and golloped up the last in the line . . . And the second last . . . And the third last . . . And now its hot breath was singe-ing the ends of the dachshunds' tails. 'Wow, wow, wow!' cried Sugar and Spice and 'Ow, ow, ow!' cried the children. 'Save us, help us, we're all going to be gobbled up . . .!'

There came no answer – only the gentle shush-shush of the sea, singing its lullaby. But the shush-shush seemed to grow louder and become a plash-plash – the plash-plash of oars; and through the plash-plash of the oars came muffled cries of

'Ow, dang!' and 'Dar she blows!' and there was the crumbling sound of a lifeboat's keel running up on to the sand, and out of the lifeboat tumbled a horde of little men in yellow macs, running this way and that, their heads tilted well back to avoid being totally blinded by their huge yellow sou'westers. 'Dar she be!' they cried, their voices muffled in yellow macintosh. 'Monster a-hoy!' 'Yes, it *is* a-hoy!' cried the children. 'It's a-hoying along behind us like anything, we'll soon all be gobbled up.' '*We*'ll save ye, *we*'ll save ye!' cried the little men and went dashing off back to the boat. 'Where be bait?' They evidently couldn't find the bait (though when they finally did, it was large enough) – and there were great cries of 'Ow, dang!' and 'Dar she blows!' and finally, blowing indeed and with a good deal of 'ow, danging' on her own behalf, Evangeline was hauled out from the bottom of the boat and triumphantly carried up the beach, two little yellow men to each stout arm and leg, and lots more bent double under her middle. There was a strong smell of scorching as the monster breathed one last breath on the dachshunds' tails, and then it had turned away. The lifeboat men laid the sacrifice reverently on a large black rock and scuttled like a cluster of huge yellow beetles, back to the safety of their boat.

'Oh, *lor'*!' said the children, uncomfortably. After all, poor Evangeline! But they went on running. Well, they *couldn't* stop – could they?

The monster advanced purposefully upon its prey: and came to a halt. For from behind a rock, out stepped a dark figure, clad in a plaid rug, with

one commanding hand held high. 'Mine, I think?' said the Reverend Tomlinson-Seal; and added with rather less dignity: '*I* saw her first.'

'Mine,' said the monster, breathing fire.

The Reverend looked respectfully at the fire. 'It would save us a lot of trouble,' he said, thoughtfully. 'No rubbing sticks and finding pots and pans and all that.' He looked at the sea-monster, loving him as his neighbour. 'Suppose we settle for that, and share?' Cooked or raw, he added, it was all the same to him; but his dear Mmmmmglummmba-Mmmmm-glummmbans had always preferred it grilled. Medium rare? he suggested, civilly.

Oh, *poor* Evangeline! thought the children. What can we do? And they set up a shrill hubbub. 'A comet, a comet!' they cried in chorus, pointing to the empty sky and the empty sea. 'An octopus, a simply huge, horrible octopus!'

'I don't care for octopusses,' said the Reverend Seal, uneasily, glancing out over the water. 'Nor I for comets,' agreed the monster, rolling in his tongue and looking anxiously upwards. The children redoubled their efforts. 'An octopus! A comet!'

And sure enough, floating in on the waves came a terrible creature of net and straw with tentacles of draggled wet veiling and all covered with lumps of sodden pink artificial roses; and across the moon's face floated a bright object trailing streamers of rich brown false hair.

'Ow-ow,' said Mr Seal, uncertainly, in a somewhat barking voice; and 'Ow-*ow*,' said the sea-monster, not at all happily either: ceaseless ow-ow-owing had been coming all this time from the hapless Evangeline, spread-eagled upon her rock. 'If we were very quick,' suggested the monster, 'and didn't fuss too much about the cooking—?'

'Smangle-himble-umbringle-tum-crumble-bump,' said the Reverend Seal, which in Mmmmmglummmba – Mmmmmglummmban means, 'O.K.'

A white-coated figure came up to them, quietly. It was the keeper from the aquarium. 'Whatever are you a-doing-of here?' he said to the Reverend Seal. 'You come on back along a' me, to where you belongs.'

'Scrimble-hum-plop-stunk-from-brandle-stropping-tum,' said the Reverend Seal, which in Mmmmmglummmba-Mmmmmglummmban means, 'No.'

'Oh, yes, you will,' said the keeper. 'You too,' he added to the sea-monster. 'You'll suit our place fine.'

The monster rolled out his tongue and shot out

a little flame but he did it rather half-heartedly. 'Nothing of the sort,' he said; and together they advanced upon Evangeline.

The keeper said nothing, simply turned his back on them. Across the top of his bald head was written in large black letters: THEN YOU'RE BOTH SILLY OLD FOOLS! He glanced meaningfully out across the dark water and up to the moonlit sky.

Mr Seal and the monster went with him quietly, without another word. Evangeline struggled up from her rock; her usually red round face was now rather white, though, fortunately, as usual practically invisible under her large, round, droopy hat. Sugar and Spice civilly made way for her so that they could run behind and nip Pug; and off they all started again. They ran and they ran and they ran . . .

They were terribly hungry – and terribly thirsty. 'If we could only stop for a minute!' cried the poor children. 'If there was only something to eat and drink!' – and even as they said it, there appeared just ahead, two thin figures standing in a hip-bath – or rather not so much standing as marching up and down with a tremendous swinging of arms and raising of curiously purple

knees; though they appeared to be getting nowhere at all. 'Fiddle! Miss Fizzle!' cried the children. 'What are you doing in that hip-bath?' 'Treading grapes,' cried Fizzle and Fiddle in unison. 'Wine,' cried the children. 'Wine! Give us some wine!' 'We can't stop,' said Fizzle and Fiddle, 'or the jelly-fishes will slide off our heads.' And it was true that on each head was a jelly-fish, delicately wobbling as the ladies soldiered on.

Podge Green came running to meet them. 'Rice pudding, rice pudding!' he cried, holding up aloft a huge pillow-case, bulging with it; and indeed his fat, round face was covered with it too. Even for rice pudding, they would have given all they had; but when they tried to call out to him, all of a sudden their mouths were full of whistle and they could only go, 'Whew-whew-wheeeeeew!' and Sugar and Spice and Pug thought they were whistling to them, broke ranks, advanced upon Podge, who dropped the pillow-case in terror at being set upon by such fearsome beasts and stood aside while they gollopped up the lot. Hardly able to stagger, they resumed their places at the end of the long line of children with Evangeline, Podge Green now with them too: and which of the five wobbled most when they ran, it would be very hard to say.

They came to a sign-post. PUDDLETON-ON-SEA it said, pointing back the way they had come; but the other sign said TO LITTLE PIDDLINGTON and pointed onwards. 'A town!' cried the children, forging wretchedly ahead, their legs hardly able to move, but powering on like little engines, just the same. 'There'll be something to eat and drink in a town.' And sure enough, soon their feet found the hard surface of a proper road instead of soft, white sand and ahead of them they saw the dark outline of houses, with a narrow street running between. But all the windows were blank, like closed eyes, still asleep; and when they knocked at the doors, voices cried, 'Go away! You've got the wrong lodgings, this is OCEAN VIEW, this is SANDYBANKS, this is the HAPPYHOLME BOARDING HOUSE – you've got us mixed up, *you* want LIBERTY HALL . . .'

They caught up with a crocodile of boys, creeping in the dawn, unwillingly to school. 'Join in with the boys,' they cried, all down along the line, 'we may get some breakfast when they reach the school!' But the master came swish, swish, swish with his cane across their stumbling legs. 'Go away, go away!' he cried. 'I know what you want, you want lobster, but you shan't have any, shell-fish is bad for you, you'll see boys before your eyes.' The children could not help rather hoping that the sea-monster was at this moment seeing boys before his eyes after all the crab he had eaten, shells and the lot; but no doubt that would in fact be delicious for him, especially if the boys were fat, so they un-wished it again; and anyway, they had enough to think about for themselves.

They passed a little station. 'A train!' they cried. 'A train will take us home!' And indeed a train was standing in the station, its engine sending up a shower of dancing sparks into the early morning dark. But a voice cried, through a foghorn, 'Allstationsto *Woant*hurt, *Ly*still, *Bee*sick and *Bed*pan . . . All change at *Big*dose, *Little*pill and Wantergotterthe*loo* . . . ' And none of those stations was home. The children had to run on.

Chapter 8

HEY ran and they ran. The sun came up and the hard road grew hot beneath their pounding feet; and when they turned off into the lanes, the hedges were thick and high, closing them in from the fresh morning air. And when they reached out, as they raced by, for the bright fruit and berries that glowed there, or only for a cool flower to lay against their burning faces and bring them a breath of sweet scent – they found that all the berries weren't berries at all, but things of paste and paint, and the flowers weren't real flowers at all, but bits of silk and twisted wire: and the ferns were feathers dyed green and the golden stems were nothing but bits of straw. They were running, running, running through lanes of preposterous great hats. 'Oh, well,' said the children, 'at least perhaps the hats

will keep the sun off our poor heads,' and they each seized a hat and clapped it on as they ran. (Yes, well, of *course* they looked silly, a long line of children running along country roads in huge old-lady hats; but it was better than sunstroke. You'd have done the same.)

On and on. The Big Ones in the lead, the Middlings trailing after them, the Littlies trailing after *them*, lugging the Tinies; Podge Green and Evangeline, wobbling along, helping one another, for Podge was somewhat blinded by the rice pudding on his face, and Evangeline by the floppy round hat. Sugar and Spice and Pug brought up the rear, without even the energy to nip. 'Oh, for some food!' they all cried. 'Oh for something to drink!' Even Podge and Evangeline and Pug and the dachshunds had got over the rice pudding and could have done with something more. Only Miss Prawn's mother was happy and comfortable, munching away at her soap as poor Prawnie, chilblains glowing, galloped along beside the children, propelling the foaming bath-chair.

They came to a village and now the windows were open and lights were on and from the fried fish shop came the most delicious aromas. 'Oh, give us some fish!' cried the children. 'Please, please give us some fish!' And lo and behold! who should appear in the doorway but Mrs Bloggs from the hospital, carrying a great big bucket; and she dipped her hand into the bucket and started throwing fish to them. But as she threw, she began to spin, dizzily, round and round in little circles, quite scarlet in the face with high temperature, and buzzing away happily to herself; and as she spun, the fish flew wide; and there appeared on the far side of the road a huge wooden table and all the fish went flop, flop, flop under the table; and were glued there to the under-side.

And the empty pail rolled out into the road, and to add to her miseries, the wretched Prawn got one foot stuck in it; and clattered dreadfully as she hopped and hobbled along behind the bath-chair. 'We must get her to a hospital,' said the children among themselves, 'and have it wrenched off, if only to stop this terrible noise.'

But at the hospital, the nurses were all tied together by their apron strings, a great octopus mass, struggling to get free: and when the children tried to untie them, running round them

in small circles, each taking a tug at an apron string as they passed, they saw that the hospital was guarded by very fierce animals in cages made of upside-down cots; and that the animals were extremely likely to break free. 'Ow, ow!' cried the children, rather anxiously. 'Help, help!'

'We'll help you, we'll help you,' cried a dozen voices; and a fleet of old gentlemen came surging down the hospital steps. They looked very odd, for some of them were in dressing-gowns much too small, with their poor thin sick legs showing miles of striped pyjama, and some of them in dressing-gowns much too large, stumbling over the hems of them as they ran. But still they were coming to help; only now the children saw that they were tied tight to the ends of their beds by the cords of their dressing-gowns, and towing the beds behind them. And the beds all got stuck in the doorway of the hospital and a terrible traffic jam ensued: and leaping from bed to bed in a sort of tribal dance was a stout old gentleman whose pyjama top flew wide, showing a tummy, dyed to a brilliant blue. But as he danced, he carried on one hand, like a waiter, high above his head a hospital supper tray: and the tray was laden with thick soup, steak and kidney puddings and plum duff.

'Oh, Mr Stout,' cried the children, 'give it to us, give it to us! It's our favourite meal!' But round the corner came whizzing in an invalid chair, an angry old lady, also brightly blue. 'Nonsense, nonsense, give it to *me*!' she cried. 'I've been out for an airing, I'm frozen, I need to be warmed up.' 'Oh, Mrs Chumping,' cried the children, 'we didn't know they meant an air-ring; we were trying to be kind!' But Mrs Chumping only growled at them almost as fiercely as the animals and they couldn't wait any longer, they had to run on.

A line of empty cabs came ambling by. 'Rescue, rescue!' cried the children and sure enough the cabs stopped and they all climbed in. But the floors of the cabs had been taken out and they found themselves running as much as ever; indeed the drivers would have whipped up their horses and run the children almost off their feet, but the horses remembered their kindness, perhaps, and refused to move faster. So they all scrambled out again; and when a fleet of bath-chairs caught up with them, they didn't even bother: which was just as well, for the chairs were filled with angry old ladies and gentlemen bleating out for the youth-giving properties of a covering of whipped white of egg . . .

The long day passed – the long, long, weary day: and they had been running since last night, when the stars had come out and sparkled in the deep blue velvet of the evening sky. Now it was hot afternoon; and it should have been tea time, only there was no tea. They thought about the possibility of cake in the hats they had picked from the hedgerows; but the seagulls had thought of that first, and no cake was there. And then . . .

And then . . .

They breasted a hill; their poor tired legs just slowly grinding along like little piston engines, their tummies aching, their throats dry with thirst . . . And there in a meadow on the other side of the hill, was the strangest sight. For it had been snowing. Just in that meadow alone, it had been snowing, and all the ground was white – as white as the tablecloth laid out in the middle of the meadow, laden with good things to eat – with ham sandwiches and jam sandwiches, and every kind of cake; with a great brown teapot in the middle and jugs of milk and sugar-basins heaped high. And sitting all round the picnic, in their good serge dresses and their good flannel petticoats and their high button boots, were Great-Aunt Adelaide Stitch and Mrs Grobble and Mrs Guttziz and Mrs Rumbletum and all the other ladies, wearing each other's hats. 'Oh, Aunt Adelaide,' cried the children, 'oh, Mrs Grobble, oh, Mrs Guttziz, oh, Mrs Rumbletum! – we're so hot and tired and thirsty, do please give us something to eat!' But the ladies sat motionless in their chairs. 'We can't,' they said.

'Can't?' said the children, still running, but running round the picnic now, and the ladies and the chairs, in a sort of Red Indian circle.

'Why not?'

'We're stuck,' said the ladies; and now that the children looked closer they saw that indeed the ladies did seem fixed rather tightly in the deck chairs and in very curious positions indeed. 'The

canvas has slit,' they said, 'and we've all got stuck.'

A sort of vague, vague memory began to come back to the children. Had they not, long, long, long ago before the world was just a place for running through – hadn't they got stuck in those very deck chairs? Hadn't they been stuck there, looking up at the moonlit night, listening to the shush-shush lullaby of the sea and longing to go to sleep; and staying wide awake . . .? And – falling asleep at last. But what had they been saying, just before they fell asleep . . .?

And the children positively stopped running; and standing in a ring round the picnic laid out on the snowy ground, said to one another, their hot, flushed faces growing pale: 'The Baby! All this time the Baby hasn't been with us. Where is the Baby?'

And a voice said, with a shake in it: 'Yes, what's happened to the Baby?' And a voice said with a break in it: 'All this time we've been thinking about our tired legs and our empty tummies – and forgotten all about the Baby . . .' And a voice said with tears in it: 'We've been selfish and beastly, just worrying about ourselves, and never even given a thought to our own poor Baby . . .'

And suddenly – everything began to happen at once: for the whole white picnic tablecloth seemed to have come alive. Cups and saucers flew up in the air and came down with a crash, cake and sandwiches flung themselves about as though, beneath the snow, a volcano had erupted; the teapot streamed hot brown tea, the milk jugs streamed cold white milk, the cakes and sandwiches were split to smithereens. And Great-Aunt Adelaide Stitch rose up and out of her chair and streaked off across the snowy field as fast as her thin old legs would carry her; and after her went Mrs Grobble and Mrs Guttziz and Mrs Rumbletum and all the other ladies, and with *them* went Miss Prawn, clankety-clank with her bucket on her foot, great cries of protest coming from the soap-lathered bath-chair. And Podge and Evangeline detached themselves from the ring of staring children and lit out after them, and Sugar and Spice gave one last loving nip as Pug's curly stump of a tail disappeared after *them*. And a voice said: 'Oh, my naughty children – my wicked, wicked ones! – I was beginning to wonder when you'd be kind again.'

And Nurse Matilda stood there with the baby safe in her loving arms: in her long black skirt and her rusty black jacket and her little black bonnet, all trembly with jet – and her face was so lovely that all the children cried out: 'Oh, Nurse Matilda – how pretty, how *pretty* you look!'

If only it hadn't been for that one huge tooth sticking straight out over her lower lip!

And Nurse Matilda smiled; and she lifted up

her big black stick and gave one gentle tap with it on the snowy meadow grass. And out flew the tooth and landed in the snow, at the children's feet.

And it began to grow. It grew and it grew. It grew until it was the size of a matchbox. It grew until it was the size of a snuff-box. It grew until it was the size of a shoe-box – of a tuck-box – of a suitcase – of a packing case – of a trunk, of a big trunk, of a simply enormous trunk. And all the while, as it grew it was taking shape; growing tall and curved, growing painted and shining, growing curly painted patterns on the shining paint: growing little curtained windows, growing big yellow wheels, growing shafts, growing a stout brown horse between the shafts, growing little steps up to a little painted door . . . And all the children cried out: 'It's a bathing machine! It's a painted bathing machine!'

But it wasn't: it was a caravan, a gypsy caravan, much, much bigger and brighter and gayer than any bathing machine. And, carrying the baby, Nurse Matilda went up the little steps and ducked through the little painted door; and all the children went in, crowded in, pushing and piling in and yet

each seeming to find a comfortable place with lots of room: all clustered round Nurse Matilda as she sat in the centre of the painted wooden seat, curled up around her, wearily, safely, tired-out from their long, long journey; dropping off to sleep around her, one by one, like drowsy bees in a bright-painted honey-pot. And clip-clop-clip went the hooves of the stout brown horse, and nid-nod, nid-nod went the weary heads . . . And there came a big gate – but it wasn't the gate of the Puddleton sea-side hotel; and a curving drive up to a big front door, standing wide. And smiling down on them were the welcoming, open windows of their own dear home!

And – how could it have happened that to each child it seemed as if loving arms came around him and he was lifted up gently and his weary head cradled against a kind shoulder? And he was carried softly and silently into the house and up the wide stairs and put down carefully in the safety of the dear old nursery-schoolroom at home . . .

And suddenly, they were all wide awake; wide awake and sitting round the big old schoolroom table, with the sunshine pouring in at the open windows – and Nurse Matilda was saying: 'Now you must write your bread-and-butter letter to your Great-Aunt Adelaide . . .' So they clustered round the table and earnestly wrote the letter. 'Dere Great-Arnt Adelaide,' said the letter, 'Thank yuo very much for haveing us to stay at the sea side after we came out of hospidilt . . .'

But when they had come to the end of the letter, and had dutifully sent love to Avangeleen and Pug and Fiddle and Miss Prorn, and had time to look up – the Baby was sitting in its high chair beating cheerfully on a plate with its silver spoon – but Nurse Matilda was gone.